Doug enjoyed creating situations that would bring his mother pain.

A shiny new buggy rolled into the yard and stopped at the hitching rail. . . .

Hattie motioned with her head. "Looks like Mr. Doug bought himself a new buggy." She continued toward the kitchen door and then stopped. Mouth opened, eyes wide, Hattie stared.

The same expression covered Mary Lou's face.

Brazenly hanging on Doug's arm was a girl from the saloon! Mary Lou couldn't believe it. . . .His mother would be shocked!

. . .Allena entered the kitchen as the front door banged. . .

Doug strutted in, the girl slightly behind him and noticeably uneasy. He. . .looked at Allena. "Mother, this is my wife, Lily." He pulled the girl from behind him and thrust her forward. "Sorry we didn't have time for her to change from her wedding gown."

Allena raised to her full height and nodded slowly.

The new bride wore a short, flouncy ruffled dress and high-heeled, lacy shoes. A black Spanish fringed shawl covered her bare shoulders, the ends clutched tightly in her hands. . . .

Allena hesitated only a second. . .she graciously stepped forward and stretched both hands toward her new daughter-in-law.

NORENE MORRIS was born, as she says, "with a pencil in my hand." Morris made her inspirational fiction debut in the Heartsong Presents series with *Cottonwood Dreams*.

Books by Norene Morris

HEARTSONG PRESENTS
HP12—Cottonwood Dreams

Rainbow Harvest

Norene Morris

A sequel to **Cottonwood Dreams**

Heartsong Presents

To my rainbow harvest,
Sharleen, Paula, and Allen

ISBN 1-55748-411-2

RAINBOW HARVEST

one

Tom Langdon pulled his wagon to a stop at the edge of the Red River. "This is where we cross. It's fairly shallow here. The bottom's bumpy, so hold on. Better steady Dulcie. Tinder's used to it, but it might frighten her."

Tom eased the front wheels into the water. The wheels sank into the reddish-brown clay. Mary Lou grabbed her seat with one hand, pulled the rope tied to Dulcie with the other, and coaxed her wild-eyed horse to enter. Dulcie's nostrils flared, her front hoofs dug into the mud, and she backed from the water.

"Come on, Dulcie, you're all right. Nothing to be afraid of. Easy, girl." Mary Lou wasn't quite sure who she was encouraging, her horse or herself. She pulled hard on the rope that tied Dulcie to the wobbly wagon and forced her into the water that slowly crept halfway up the wheels.

Dulcie laid her ears back and followed the familiar voice.

Mary Lou glanced admiringly at her fearless new husband. Feet braced, he maneuvered the struggling team and swaying wagon across the river. When wheels rolled onto the other side, Tinder and Dulcie splashed past the wagon to dry land. Mary Lou heaved a relieved sigh and smiled at Tom.

He leaped to the ground and lifted Mary Lou down to soothe Dulcie. Tinder trotted to Tom and nuzzled his arm. "Good boy! You're getting to be an old hand at this." Tom inspected the dripping wagon and team, climbed aboard, handed Mary Lou back up into her seat, and flipped the reins around his knee. He pulled her to him and kissed her. "Well, Mrs. Langdon. Welcome to Texas!"

His enfolding arms brought instant calm. Mary Lou warmed in her husband's gaze, returned his kiss, then adjusted her bonnet to shield her face from the late afternoon sun. Ahead, a distant copse of trees enticed her with its fan of precious shade.

"Crossing the river means we're close to home." Tom patted Mary Lou's hand and pointed to the trees. "They're about two miles away. We can rest and get some shade." Mary Lou heaved a sigh and smiled gratefully.

"If we pushed, we could make it home by nightfall," he added.

Panic rose in Mary Lou's throat. Her lips parted for a quick intake of breath. Tom's home—the place she eagerly anticipated seeing, yet feared. A bubbling undercurrent of excitement overrode momentary alarm and flooded her mind with indescribable joy. Home—where she and Tom would begin their life together.

All the way from Kansas, Tom had proudly described the Circle Z until Mary Lou's mind pictured a rambling adobe ranch, horse and cattle barns, corrals, bunkhouse, amiable cowboys, and the majestic beauty of the surrounding land. Hearing him talk about his father's fierce love of the land, Mary Lou recognized Tom had inherited that love. He spoke with purpose and pride, eager to get home and show it to her.

"There's a fair-sized stream winding in those trees—a good place to camp for the night, rest, and clean up. What do you think?"

"I'd like that." Mary Lou relaxed. "Maybe I could wash my hair. Meeting your family tomorrow, I'd like to look my best."

Tom leaned over and kissed her again. "All they're going to see is the beautiful bride I brought home. After they get to know you, they'll love you as I do."

Mary Lou hoped so.

Lying awake beside Tom, long after her husband's breathing told her he slept, Mary Lou prayed for her new family. In her mind, they'd become life-and-blood people.

Tom spoke of his mother with loving admiration—called her a strong Christian woman. And Nelson. Mary Lou could hardly wait to meet Tom's youngest brother and see his beautiful paintings. Tom held an obvious pride in his oldest brother, Zackary. She wondered about Zack's new wife, Darcy. Tom hadn't said much except that she was from the East and was not too happy with ranch life. He'd spoken briefly of his older brother, Doug. "He needs lots of prayer," was all he had said. Not knowing exactly what to pray for, Mary Lou simply lifted Doug's name to God.

Her heart tugged her back home to her father. She couldn't help grieving at his disapproval of Tom and his refusal to come and say good-bye when they left. As always, the memory of Mama's sweet spirit reminded Mary Lou of God's willingness to listen to His children's problems. "Lord," Mary Lou prayed, "I thought Pa'd forgiven me, but marrying Tom made him angry again. I don't know what to do anymore. It would all be so different if Mama were still alive."

"If your father isn't happy about it, that's his problem, not yours. Now, go—with God's blessing." Aunt Tibby's parting words echoed in Mary Lou's mind and soothed her.

This would be Tom and Mary Lou's last night alone under the dark, friendly sky that kindly provided a blanket of twinkling stars and a warm quiet breeze. As much as she looked forward to the comforts of the ranch, Mary Lou cherished this time when they belonged only to each other. Hereafter, they would be surrounded by Tom's family.

Wide awake, Mary Lou gazed into her husband's sleeping face, his copper-topped head cradled on one arm. He looked as vulnerable as a small boy, but at their wedding Tom had proved himself a true Christian gentleman, even to Glenn. The two men had shaken hands and parted friends though Mary Lou had almost married Glenn.

Tom stirred, opened dreamy eyes, and caught Mary Lou's loving gaze. His mouth bent into a sleepy grin. "Come here, wife," he said huskily and gathered her into his arms.

Wife! The new truth permeated her innermost being. Home would always be wherever Tom is. She snuggled closer and surrendered mind and body to loving him.

The dusty buckboard rattled under the Circle Z arch around one o'clock. Nelson, behind an easel on the porch, grabbed his crutches and stood, cautious and curious.

Tom waved and hollered, "Nelson, it's me."

Nelson spun on one crutch, called through the open door, and bounced along at surprising speed toward the approaching wagon. In the doorway, a woman appeared, paused, then came running.

When they met, Tom jumped out and threw his arms around his mother and brother, then lifted Mary Lou to his side. Nelson's winsome face beamed with expectancy.

Mary Lou took to Nelson immediately, just as Tom had said she would. She smiled at his mother and steadied herself against Tom's shoulder, apprehension fluttering her stomach.

Mrs. Langdon stood tall and regal. The sun sparked silver highlights on her crown of red-bronze hair.

Tom put his arms around Mary Lou. "Mother, this is Mary Lou—Langdon."

Allena Langdon's eyes widened in surprise and stared. *Oh, Lord, let her accept me,* Mary Lou prayed.

Allena regarded her new daughter-in-law with raised brows, then stepped forward graciously, clasped Mary Lou's shoulders with firm, gentle hands, and planted a kiss on her cheek. "Now I know why Tom was so eager to leave on this year's cattle drive." She turned to her grinning son. "I should have known you'd find yourself a beauty."

Tom grinned. "Was I that obvious?"

"I knew there was something you weren't telling me." She turned to Mary Lou and held out both hands. "Welcome home, Mrs. Langdon."

Mrs. Langdon! Mary Lou's heart flooded with gratitude to this kind woman whose eyes sparkled clear and honest like Mama's. "Thank you. I'm glad to be—home."

Allena's arm encircled Mary Lou's small waist. "You must be tired, child. That's a long, hard trip. Come with me and we'll see what we can do to Tom's room to make it proper for a bride. Hattie can make us some tea and rustle up something to eat."

They stepped inside the ranch house door. Its coolness surprised Mary Lou. They walked through a spacious and airy main room with an Indian blanket hanging on one wall and small rugs of similar design scattered on the floor in front of rugged furniture. Simple. Homey. She gazed with delight at the intensely alive Texas landscapes that dominated the walls. At any moment, she expected balls of tumbleweed to escape their confining frames and bounce into the room. Had Nelson painted these?

Down the hall at the far end of the house, Tom's room held a large bed, a bureau, and a wash stand. More Indian rugs dotted the floor. A breeze fluttered homespun curtains at the windows.

"The men will unload the wagon. Until they come, you and I can get acquainted." Allena sat on the bed and patted for Mary Lou to sit beside her.

Mary Lou's heart pounded in her ears. She'd never felt

more alone. She wasn't afraid of Tom's mother—her tender greeting had erased that. Could she live up to be the wife Mrs. Langdon wanted for her son?

"Tell me about yourself and your family," her mother-in-law asked. Mary Lou described her father's general store and how she and her mother had worked in the post office. Her words stopped when she spoke of Mama's death. A gentle hand grasped her shoulder. Another lifted her chin.

Allena Langdon reached into her apron pocket and gently daubed Mary Lou's moist eyes with a hankie that carried the fragrance of fresh wind.

Mary Lou sniffed, swallowed, and continued. "That's why I became postmistress and how I met Tom. Every day he came either to post a letter or to pick up mail for his men."

Allena nodded and smiled. "You're shedding light on a lot of my questions. I'd never received as many letters from Tom on any previous cattle drive. Tom is a Texas boy at heart and loves his ranch. I just thought he was homesick."

Mary Lou closed her eyes. Her mind filled with delicious remembering. "I loved him the first day he walked into the post office and our hands brushed when he handed me a letter."

Allena's face spread with pleasant surprise. "Same as Tom's father and me. Zackary asked me to dance a square with him at a barn dance when I was fourteen. When our hands touched it was magic." Allena's voice faded and her gaze hung on a faraway memory.

"You must have loved him very much," Mary Lou said softly.

"He was my life—the only man I'll ever love. He gave me four sons and enough good years for a lifetime." Allena gathered within herself, lost in memories. "When Zackary died, I transferred my love to them."

Surprisingly, Allena laughed. "Sometimes I'm too much mother hen for their liking, but I'll let go when they each find their love." She paused, then commented aloud, as if to herself. "But I have Nelson. I hope he can marry someday. If not, we have our painting."

So that's where Nelson inherited his talent. Being alone with her new mother-in-law these few moments sent tingling excitement through Mary Lou. Had God moved again to give her not only the blessing of a good husband, but a new mother and brothers and sister as well?

Mary Lou continued the story of her betrothal to Glenn. "After Mama died, Glenn was gentle and caring. His attentions eased my pain, especially when I received no letters from Tom. I finally gave up ever seeing Tom again. Glenn and I worked together in the store. I still love him as a friend, but I wanted Tom for my husband."

Allena laughed. "So that's why Tom wrote letters and tore them up!"

Mary Lou's heart leaped. Tom had told her he had wanted to write but didn't dare. One by one, things settled into place and made sense. She laughed. "Poor Tom. When he came back I was betrothed and couldn't talk to him because we women in Venture had formed a Women's Christian Temperance Union, had smashed the saloon, and weren't speaking to the men until they moved the saloon to the outskirts of town."

"Good for you! You've got spunk. A rancher's wife needs the strength of two women to survive Texas."

"Or Kansas."

Allena squeezed Mary Lou's hand and nodded. "I've a hunch you'll make it. Zack looks like his father, but Tom has his father's heart and needs a real woman for a wife, not a little girl."

Touched, Mary Lou swallowed a lump that rose in her throat.

"You may find people around here a bit rough at first," Allena continued, "but inside most are good, kind, solid Americans trying to cut a life for themselves out of this harsh wilderness." Allena fixed her gaze on Mary Lou. "If it's not too soon, I'd be proud if you'd call me Mother."

Mary Lou relaxed. Feeling no disrespect for Mama's memory, she leaned toward Mrs. Langdon. "Thank you—Mother." The last vestige of fear of Tom's mother took wings.

When Mary Lou related the crazy confusion of the wedding, the two Mrs. Langdons laughed so hard that tears came. Until that moment, Mary Lou hadn't appreciated the humor of the situation.

The thump of boots resounded down the hall. Tom appeared in the doorway, his arms loaded. "What's going on in here?"

Allena and Mary Lou exchanged knowing glances.

"Just woman stuff," Allena said, rising to accept an armful of quilts.

Mary Lou sprang to help. They found space for Mama's dresser, rocking chair, and small table. Mary Lou unwrapped Aunt Tibby's lamp.

Allena gasped with pleasure. "Haven't seen anything this pretty since I was a little girl back in North Carolina. I have a small one of my mother's but nothing as grand as this." Allena turned the lamp round and round.

Mary Lou inwardly thanked Aunt Tibby. "Can't send you off to your mother-in-law like a poor relation," she'd said. Her aunt had been right, as usual.

They unrolled her mother's lovely quilts and Henrietta's lace tablecloth. Allena oohed and aahed over each one and smoothed them with her hands.

Mary Lou lifted the lamp and surveyed the room. "I don't know where I'd put this in here. It's too fancy for a bedroom. Mother, could you use it in the parlor?"

Allena was jubilant. "Thank you, my dear. I've just the place for it." She flashed Tom an appreciative smile. Lamp held high, she carried it carefully out the door and disappeared.

Tom's gaze carried his love across the room. He pushed the door shut with his boot and took Mary Lou in his arms. "You'll never know how many times I've dreamed of this moment. You—here, with me—my wife." Tom held her tenderly and whispered into her hair, "I thank God for you."

His kiss ignited a flare of happiness that warmed her whole being. She relaxed. Home at last.

Shortly after everyone gathered for the noon meal, Zack's booming voice announced he and Darcy were home from Harness. He seated Darcy and spied Tom. "You're back! I wondered who that buckboard belonged to."

The brothers affectionately slapped each other on the back.

"Zack, this is Mary Lou, my wife."

Zack stared in surprise then threw back his head and roared. "Well, I'll be. Couldn't let your big brother get ahead of you, could you?" He punched Tom's arm and walked to Mary Lou and put out his hand.

Zack's firm fingers closed over hers. His blue-black head bent, and Mary Lou crimsoned when his soft lips touched the back of her hand. He glanced up and grinned. "So you're Mary Lou. No wonder my brother was pining." Zack reached for Darcy who rose and came to Zack's side. "Mary Lou, meet my wife, Darcy."

Darcy gazed up at Zack then turned nonchalantly to Mary Lou, green eyes snapping a clear message: Zack belongs to me.

Allena's mouth opened in surprise. "You knew about Mary Lou?" Zack smacked his hands together. "For the first time in my life, Mother, I knew something before you. It's time you learned men know a lot more than we tell the ladies." Zack clasped and pumped Tom's hand. "When we talked, it seemed hopeless. I'm glad it worked out."

Allena held her hands up. "I surrender and admit my boys are grown and don't need a tagging mother any more."

Zack released himself from Darcy, crossed the room, and kissed his mother's cheek. "Mother, no one will ever take your place. You'll never be dethroned, but we're glad you've discovered your boys are now men."

Allena laughed and playfully shoved Zack toward his chair.

Mary Lou, charmed at the scene, glanced at Darcy who stood rigid, her lips tight, her dark eyes flooded with displeasure. She was beautiful—but unhappy. *How sad Darcy couldn't appreciate the love and respect Zack had for his mother,* Mary Lou thought. *Mama had always said: Watch how a man treats his mother. Most often, he'll treat his wife the same way.*

Allena lifted a serving bowl, passed it, and picked up another. "Sit down, please. Let's eat our dinner before it gets cold."

Darcy filled her plate and between bites began talking about Mrs. Cassidy, the only dressmaker in Harness. "The clumsiest woman I've ever seen. All thumbs and poking fingers. I know she has my measurements all wrong. My waist is only nineteen inches." Darcy spread her hands around her waist and pressed her fingers into her middle. "Can you imagine? She said I measured twenty-two!" She stuffed another bite into her mouth.

Around the table with Mary Lou and Darcy sat three men and an older woman. *It's probably just as strange here for her as it is for me,* Mary Lou thought. *Maybe she needs a friend her own age.* She tucked that thought in the back of her mind and picked up her fork.

two

Mary Lou's eyes opened slowly. She stared at the unfamiliar adobe ceiling. Beside her, Tom slept. She raised to one elbow and studied the features of his handsome, suntanned face, enthralled with the still unbelievable fact she was his wife.

He stirred, opened his eyes, and grinned. "Mornin' Mrs. Langdon," he drawled. Mrs. Langdon. She loved the sound of it.

Tom squinted at the window and sat up. "Is that daylight?" He bounded out of bed and grabbed his pocket watch. "Breakfast in this house is six sharp. I should have been up and out an hour ago." Tom grabbed Mary Lou's hands and pulled her out of bed into his arms. "See what you do to me, woman? I forget everything."

Mary Lou snuggled to stay, but Tom released her and hurried into his clothes. She washed, slipped into a blue calico, brushed and braided her long, chestnut hair, and wrapped the braid around her head. She sensed Tom watching her as she dressed, and flushed at the tender, amused expression on his face. When she finished, he gathered her into his arms, kissed her, and nuzzled her neck. "I love you," he whispered before he released her and swung the door open.

As usual, Allena sat in her place waiting. Tom held Mary Lou's chair, and she slipped into it. Meticulously dressed in the latest fashion, Darcy followed Zack into the dining room.

"Good morning, Darcy, Zack," Mary Lou said cheerily.

Darcy nodded slightly and slid into the chair Zack held for her.

The Langdon men had dignity and manners. Mary Lou glanced with admiration at Allena, who sat like a queen on a throne, patiently waiting for her subjects to settle.

Alert and smiling, Nelson greeted everyone.

What a dear boy. In spite of his handicap, he was undaunted. Mary Lou made an inward promise to find time to talk with him, tell him how much she loved his paintings, and see more of them.

"Tom, say grace, please." Allena bowed her head.

When Tom finished, Mary Lou gazed across the table at Doug's empty chair, curious about this brother she hadn't met. He hadn't appeared the night before for supper. Allena was visibly disturbed by his absence. During the night, Mary Lou vaguely remembered shuffling and whispering in the hall. Had that been Doug?

"Doug's late again," Zack commented.

"Doug had an early breakfast and left for Harness." Allena sipped her coffee. "Said he had business to take care of."

A frown creased Zack's brow. "He needs to run this ranch on the ranch instead of from ten miles away." His voice betrayed his irritation. He avoided his mother's gaze. "A lot of repairs need to be done. Father would be appalled."

"I agree with you," Allena said. "I know it, Tom knows it, Smitty and the cowboys know it. Why do you think I wrote you to come home?" Like a mother hen sparring for an attacked chick, she threw a challenge. "Why don't you and Tom take the responsibility of repairs and fix what's needed with help from the boys? It's your ranch, too, you know. Doug has carried the load since your father died and you left for law school. He could use some help."

Zack leaned against the back of his chair and met his mother's indignant stare. "Doug refuses to let loose any ranch business or discuss it. He avoids us by running to town. Mother, I haven't seen one record ledger. Tom and I should have access to them as well as Doug." His jaw flexed. A knowing look passed between him and Tom. "Either he does a better job—and soon—or there'll have to be some drastic changes around here to save the ranch."

"Save the ranch!" Allena straightened and paled.

"Yes. I've checked on some land dealings and...." Zack leaned over his plate and stuffed a forkful of steak into his mouth.

Allena stiffened. "And?"

Zack chewed, swallowed, then met his mother's demanding gaze. "It looks as if part of the Circle Z has been sold."

"Sold! Who? When?"

"Mother, right now Doug is the only one except me with legal authority to sell any land, and I haven't been here."

Allena gasped and her eyes filled with pain. She shook her head. "Doug wouldn't!"

"I haven't solid proof yet, but at least a quarter of the land in the far south acreage may be sold."

"To whom?"

"I'm not sure. I'm guessing land speculators from the East. I've seen several in Harness. But everything is shady, and I'm having a hard time pinning down facts. No one wants to talk, especially to me. I don't have enough proof to make any accusations." Zack gazed tenderly at his mother. "I suspect Doug is selling off the land to pay his gambling debts. He owes everybody in town."

Mary Lou watched the proud woman shrivel in her chair. Her life and pride rested in her four boys. Gambling was bad enough, but selling off their inheritance to do it was beyond belief.

Suddenly, Darcy sat indignantly erect. "Then the quarter he sold is his quarter. Why don't you just disown him?"

Allena glared in shock at her daughter-in-law. "He's my son!"

"But if he's already sold his quarter and sells more—that means he'll sell Zack's land. . . ." Darcy's voice faltered under the mortified scowl of her husband. "And Tom's. And Nelson's," she added. Wilting before five astounded faces, she sputtered, "It isn't. . .fair."

"Nor is it fair to accuse a brother when we don't know all the facts." Zack's glare pursed Darcy's lips, and she stared petulantly at him like a falsely rebuked child.

"In my search," Zack continued, "I discovered two land

titles and deeds with vague descriptions of the southeast quarter of the Circle Z. There are wide discrepancies and confusing land boundaries, but they look like a blend of Langdon and Shepard property. Some of Will's cowhands were out hunting strays and reported strangers camped in two covered wagons who looked like they were settling in. Will is coming this morning, and we're going to investigate it."

Allena raised her chin. "Until we have proof, we'll discuss it no more. What if we should accuse my son and your brother when he is innocent?"

"That's what I'm counting on, Mother, that I can find the facts that will prove Doug innocent."

Mary Lou related to Allena's pain. For Mama, it had been Pa who dampened the sunshine. For Allena, her son. Did every family have a difficult member? Mary Lou's curiosity heightened about her truant brother-in-law.

Tom rose, his mother's hurt and disappointment mirrored in his eyes. "As far as we're concerned, Doug is innocent until proven guilty, and we'll treat him so." He placed his hand reassuringly on his mother's shoulder, glanced at Zack, and flashed good-bye to Mary Lou with his eyes.

Allena sternly faced her oldest son. "From now on, I want to be informed of what's going on. This is my ranch too." Her expression mixed disappointment and anguish with stoic determination.

"All right. Tom and I have stumbled across things that don't seem right. There are too many unanswered questions. We also hate to think Doug is mixed up in anything shady, but he won't talk to us about the ranch, even when we question him.

"When Will told us what his boys discovered, we thought it wise to investigate first. It could be something simple. Someone might have mistakenly moved on what he thinks is his newly purchased land. It's happened before."

Allena nodded. "What makes you think these wagons aren't the usual stopovers partaking of western hospitality? It's not unusual. Traveling wagons stop anywhere. We've had them stop here. I've found most to be good people on their way to their lands, appreciative of the chance to rest and be friendly. I've enjoyed them. Company's rare, and they bring news from back East."

Zack agreed. "But these wagons have been there over a month. Will's cowhands told us whoever it is has erected a shed and it looks like they're digging a soddie in the side of a small knoll. Will's boys wouldn't have paid any attention to a couple wagons stopped at the stream for a week or so."

"I'd like to go see."

Zack's nostrils flared. "I'd rather you didn't. It's rough riding in that quarter, and we don't know what to expect. That's why Will is bringing all the boys he can. We're taking everyone but Tex and Jess in case—"

"In case?"

"Mother, we can't take chances. If they're poachers, we need to know. If they're not, we can extend Texas hospitality for a while longer." Zack matched his mother's determined gaze.

No one had any appetite left for breakfast.

Except Darcy.

Mary Lou remained quiet. Any comment she would make would be out of place considering her new position in the family. But the thought of riding out over the land enticed her. "I'll ride with Allena," she ventured. "Tom's been so busy. . . ."

"And it'll be a good chance for Mary Lou to see some of the ranch," Allena offered.

Zack stared at his plate and stirred and restirred his coffee.

"Well then, how about if Mary Lou and I ride out a ways and then come back with Tex?" his mother coaxed.

"I want to ride, too," Darcy enjoined.

Zack stood and faced three determined women. His shoulders heaved and lowered with a resigned sigh. "All right. I'll have Tex ride and bring you back." Zack faced Darcy and anchored her with a stern expression. "On one condition. When I say you come back, you come back." He didn't wait for Darcy's answer and walked to the door. "Will said he'd be early, and we're leaving as soon as he comes. We'll wait for no one."

He turned and left, the solid thump of his boots across the kitchen placing an emphatic period on his conditions.

"Good morning, Mr. Zack," Hattie called as he passed through the kitchen. She received a slight nod of his head.

The blazing sun claimed the day and splayed its sultry

rays over the Circle Z. Even though it was early, the pulsating heat kept the men wiping their foreheads and sent cows and horses in search of available shade.

Tom, Zack, Nelson, Smitty, and half the ranch cowboys emerged from the barn, ready to mount as neighboring rancher Will Shepard, his three sons, and four cowhands rode in to meet them. A beautiful young girl with flowing blond hair, riding a frisky, dappled grey filly trotted toward the house and dismounted before Allena and Mary Lou. Allena made the introductions.

"I came to meet Tom's new wife," Laura said. "Ma said 'twas high time we paid our respects. She's been feelin' poorly. Says she'll never get used to hot Texas." She smiled at Mary Lou. "Ma's from Massachusetts." Laura plunked her hands on her hips. "So! You're the girl who stole my man."

Mary Lou's breath caught. She forced a sick smile. Then there had been something between Laura and Tom.

Laura laughed and shrugged. "Don't worry. He didn't love me. I knew it but hoped someday I'd grow up enough to make him notice me. You know how romantic young girls are about cowboys." She tossed her head. Golden curls tumbled over her shoulders and down her back. "Whew! I've got to get rid of this mop." She reached into her pocket for a ribbon and quickly tied the thick locks together at the nape of her neck.

Mary Lou stepped forward and offered her hand. "I'm glad to meet you, Laura." How could Tom have ever resisted this beautiful girl?

Allena put an arm around Laura and gave her a squeeze. "This is my shared daughter. Will and her mother, Emily, bought the land west of ours six years after Zackary and I married. We had four boys; they had three: Matthew, Mark, and Luke. Finally Emily had this girl-child. She's been generous and shares her with me." Allena turned to Laura. "We plan on riding out a ways with the men, then come back before lunch. Want to ride along?"

"Sure," exclaimed Laura. Her eyes narrowed as she looked beyond them to the ranch house. "She goin' too?"

Darcy stood on the porch dressed in a fashionable eastern riding habit. "Of course I'm going." She tossed her head and the feather plume on her hat waved back and forth.

Laura grinned and stated flatly. "You'll need that fan. You're going to bake in that outfit. There isn't much shade where we're goin'."

Mary Lou couldn't withhold a smile. Laura reminded her of Jenny, her dearest friend back in Kansas—outspoken, forthright, and alarmingly honest. Maybe. . . .

Tex appeared with their horses in tow.

Zack helped Darcy mount. She followed him to ride with the men and squeezed her horse between Zack and Will.

Tom hung back and rode with Mary Lou, Laura, and his mother.

In great delight, Nelson sat proud in the middle of the cowboys and talked incessantly.

The morning air became stifling. Mary Lou wondered

how Darcy stood the heat in her finery. She'd worn a long-sleeved calico to protect her from the sun, thankful for any small breeze, even a hot one.

An hour later, the men came to a halt. Darcy's demanding voice carried back to the other women. "But you have to take me back. I don't feel well." She jerked her elbow from Zack's hand.

It wasn't the sun that made Zack's face red. "I can't take you back. Tex will ride back with you and the others."

Darcy wailed, "But I'm sick!"

Allena rode forward. "Come, Darcy, it's an hour's ride back to the ranch. The heat is getting to me, too." Nose in the air, Darcy spoke as if to an audience. "Zack is taking me back."

Zack grabbed Darcy's reins and swung her homeward. "You're going home with Tex." His jaw muscles flexed for control. "I'm not going to argue with you." Zack softened and put his hand over hers. "Please, Darcy, if you aren't feeling well, you shouldn't be riding in this heat. This sun is much hotter than back East."

Darcy glared at Zack. Innately she sensed her surrounding audience, lifted her head and shoulders, and smiled sweetly. Her gloved hand raised and patted Zack's cheek. "I'll go, darling." Her face wilted. "But don't stay too long. I don't feel well at all."

Zack touched her hand, turned, and rode to catch up with the men. Darcy stiffened, swung her horse, slapped the reins, and took off at a gallop.

Three surprised, concerned women turned and followed.

Shortly, Darcy slowed her steed to a trot.

"Probably so hot she's about to faint," Allena said and spurred Black Beauty to catch up with her.

Mary Lou and Laura trotted side by side suppressing giggles.

Laura shook her head. "What Zack sees in her, I don't."

"He loves her," Mary Lou answered simply. "Someday the right man will come into your life, and you'll understand."

"He has come."

Mary Lou slowed. "We're not close friends yet, but would you care to tell me?"

A secret grin highlighted Laura's face. "It's Nelson."

"Nelson!"

"What's wrong with Nelson?"

"Why—nothing."

Laura's smile faded. "You think the same as Mrs. Langdon. But Nelson is nineteen, and I'll be eighteen next month."

Mary Lou's heart claimed kin to this active, charming girl. "I don't think it's age as much as a mother's concern as to how Nelson would be able to provide for a wife. How could he take care of one?"

"What's wrong with a wife to take care of him? I could run a small ranch if I had to. I've grown up with seven boys, horses, longhorns, cowboys—"

"But Nelson's—"

"Crippled? That's only his body. He has a heart, a mind,

and a beautiful spirit in that body. He's talented and could become a great artist. He could...." Laura dipped her head and tears ran free.

Mary Lou's surprise settled into admiration for this courageous, young girl who was ready to take on the whole world for the boy she loved. And here was her first real friend. *Thank You, Father. How can I help?*

three

Tom and Zack trotted Tinder and Victor under the Circle Z arch and moved into a gallop toward Harness.

Mary Lou waved until they were out of sight, then walked slowly back to the house. The main rooms were empty. She wended her way to the kitchen.

Hattie Benson stood hunched over a pan of hot, soapy water, energetically scrubbing a pot.

"May I help?"

Hattie shook her head. "No, thank you, Miss Mary. I'm near done except the few dishes on the dining table."

"I'll get them," Mary Lou said and returned to the kitchen with a tray full of dirty breakfast dishes.

"Put them on the side cupboard. I'll get to them shortly."

Mary Lou sensed faded blue eyes follow her as she wandered around the ample kitchen. A huge fireplace dominated the outside wall. Hanging pans and kettles peppered the fireplace on both sides. A hand-hewn, smoothly scrubbed table stood solidly in the center of the room. Mary Lou rubbed her hand over it. "This looks like a good place to knead dough and make bread. As a new daughter-in-law, I don't know quite what I'm supposed to do."

Hattie paused in her scrubbing and beamed. "You get

your orders from Mrs. Langdon and you can do all the bakin' you want. It's a never-endin' job keepin' up with bread, biscuits, and pies for this bunch." She bobbed her head, a wide grin spread across her tanned face. "You're gonna make Mr. Tom a good wife. Any woman who likes cookin'll take good care of her man." She glanced around quickly and lowered her voice to a giggly hoarse whisper. "An' you got the best of the four. Mr. Tom, he's special."

"I think so, too," Mary Lou whispered back, and they laughed at their little secret. Even at short acquaintance, Mary Lou admired this plain, hard-working woman crowned with a wealth of silver gray hair gathered into a tight knob. "Thank you, Mrs. Benson."

"Mrs. Benson? Call me Hattie."

"Then you call me Mary Lou."

Hattie shook her head. "No, ma'am. You're Miss Mary."

Allena entered the kitchen. "Here you are. I can see by Hattie's face you've gained her approval. How did you do it so quickly?"

"She told me she enjoyed making bread and biscuits, that's how," Hattie answered. "She asked me if it would be possible?"

"Possible?" Allena raised her brows and nodded to her new daughter-in-law. "Welcomed! Everyone in this house has to keep a hand in somewhere." Allena laughed. "Hattie lets me come out and make bread once a week so I won't lose my touch.

"Mary Lou, how would you like to ride this morning? The boys never want me to ride alone. They're concerned something might happen like the horse stepping into a hole or being spooked and throw me. My husband and I had a few rounds of disagreement 'cause I thought it was a lot of nonsense. I've ridden since I was a little girl. But after a few accidents to people around here, I decided I'd do what he asked."

Mary Lou nodded. "My pa was an excellent horseman, but one night when he was riding the line, Morgan threw him and he never rode a horse again. It changed our whole life. Yes, I'd love to ride out with you."

Allena linked arms with Mary Lou and called back over her shoulder, "Pack us a couple biscuits and some fruit, Hattie. My new daughter-in-law and I are going on a picnic!"

A dress rustled in the doorway. Darcy drooped against the frame like a pale, lost child.

"Would you like to ride with us, Darcy?" Allena asked. Darcy hesitated, then agreed.

Allena told Hattie to pack another biscuit. She turned to Darcy. "Get ready as soon as you can, dear. We want to ride out and get back before it gets too hot."

Tex brought Dulcie, Allena's Brown Beauty, and a chestnut filly named Buttons and tied them to the hitching post.

Mary Lou and Allena, ready to ride, stayed in out of the rising heat and waited for Darcy.

After ten minutes, Allena and Mary Lou walked back to Zack and Darcy's room and knocked. No answer. After another unanswered knock, Allena opened the door.

Darcy lay half-dressed on the bed. The room reeked. Both women rushed forward.

"Ohhh," moaned Darcy. "I'm sick again. Hattie must be putting something in the food."

Allena rushed to the basin and flinched. She turned to Darcy and smiled. "Darcy—are you with child?"

Darcy sat up with a jolt. "Oh, I hope not."

"You hope not?" Allena's smile faded into a frown. "Does Zack know?"

Darcy's glazed eyes flashed. "It's Zack's fault. I don't want a baby, he does." Darcy looked down at her stomach. "I can't have a baby. It'll ruin my figure!" Suddenly, Darcy leaped from the bed and fled to the basin.

Shocked, Mary Lou stared at her. How could she say such a thing? Not want a baby? Mary Lou looked forward to the time when she and Tom—

"Mary Lou, please go tell Hattie to get a couple buckets of hot soapy water and bring them here. I must clean this room."

With Hattie in tow, Mary Lou returned, each carrying a bunch of cleaning rags and steaming buckets filled to the brim.

Allena's face was white, her lips tense.

Darcy moaned and cried on the bed.

The three women scrubbed and cleaned. When they finished, Hattie fetched a pail of fresh water and a clean basin.

Allena returned to the bed. "Darcy, if you get sick, do it in the bucket, not the basin."

Darcy wailed louder.

"Do you hear what I'm saying, Darcy?"

Darcy sat up in bed, her face twisted with rage. "I hear you. But I'm not having any baby!"

"Yes you are, Darcy." Allena's voice sounded strained but stern. "This planted child not only belongs to you, it belongs to our family. I don't want to ever again hear you say you don't want it. Children are a gift, a heritage from the Lord. They are God's creation in His hands until they are born into ours. Like it or not, you happen to be carrying my first grandchild!" Allena moistened a cloth and mopped Darcy's sodden face.

Darcy shoved her hand away, her eyes snapping defiance. "Your first grandchild will ruin me and rob me. I'll never be the same again." She turned her back on Allena, buried her face in the pillow, and wailed.

Mary Lou listened in disbelief. Why was Darcy so angry? All the women she'd ever known rejoiced at the coming of a baby. At home in Venture, their neighbors, the Wimbleys, had ten children, and Henrietta joyously anticipated holding each new son or daughter in her arms. Her big heart and loving arms even gathered in Jenny and Matthew when she and Big Jon found a wrecked wagon, a bewildered little girl and a crying six-month-old boy beside dead parents. Poor Darcy. She was sick and not thinking straight. She would feel differently after the sick days were past and the baby was born. Babies had a way of changing people.

The three women stepped into the hall. Allena closed

the door, her face drained of color, her eyes brimming with tears.

What an awful thing for a mother to hear, Mary Lou thought.

"Do you still want to go for a short ride?" Allena asked. "We'll eliminate the picnic. I could use some fresh air."

Mary Lou nodded.

It felt good to be on Dulcie's back. For the first mile they ambled in a slow walk. Neither said a word. The persistent sun climbed the steps of the day, warming it considerably. Half an hour later, they dismounted to rest beside a small stream in the shade of a clump of beech trees.

Seated with her back braced against a tree, Allena swung to Mary Lou. "How do you feel about having a baby?"

Mary Lou leaned and touched Allena's arm. "I'll be delighted, and so will Tom."

Allena heaved a big sigh. "I thought so." Her gaze travelled the wide expanse of land before them. "This week has certainly been enlightening. First I hear I'm being robbed of my land by my own son, then my daughter-in-law tells me she rejects my first grandchild." Allena looked lovingly at Mary Lou. "I want you to know I'm thankful Tom picked a Christian wife. It looks like I'm going to need some prayer help."

Quite an admission from a strong woman, Mary Lou thought. "Mama said our strength comes from nothing within ourselves, but from the Lord."

"You'll have to tell me more about your mama. She

sounds like my kind of woman." Allena laid her head back against the tree trunk and closed her eyes.

Mary Lou warmed at the thought of Mama. "She loved the Lord and He ruled her whole life," she began. "I don't remember Mama beginning to read her Bible aloud to me. Every morning and evening we sat on her porch and she told and read me stories about Adam and Eve, Abraham, baby Moses, boy Samuel, and baby Jesus." Mary Lou ached in longing memory. "When Mama read the Bible, it came alive. We used to bathe and wash our hair in the stream near our cabin." She laughed. "I remember hiding behind a bush that hung out over the water pretending I was Miriam watching baby Moses floating in his basket."

A hot breeze rustled the beech leaves overhead and they danced a flickering ballet across the two women.

Mary Lou glanced at Allena. She sat motionless, her face relaxed. The younger woman continued. "It was on Mama's porch, at her knee, that I accepted Jesus as my Savior. I think I was about five." A press of tears checked more words.

The resting woman beside her stirred, opened her eyes, and smiled at Mary Lou. "You had a good mother." She studied Mary Lou's face for a long moment. "Do you think we could spend some time together in prayer early every morning?"

Mary Lou's heart swelled with gladness. She and Mama had read Scripture and prayed every morning after Pa left for the store. "Yes, I'd like that. Mama and I. . . ." The tears refused to be contained. Allena gathered Mary Lou into her arms. Young and old clung together and wept—one for a lost life and one for a life to come.

On their way back to the ranch, the two women rode silently, emotions close to the surface. The horses, sensing the release of a tight hand on the reins, headed for home and shade.

Tex came from the barn and took the horses, and the women walked leisurely to the house. Two men slowed to a trot as they rode under the Circle Z arch.

Allena paused and raised her hand to shade her eyes. "It's Doug," she exclaimed. As they drew closer she called, "Did you see Zack and Tom? They went into Harness this morning."

Doug shook his head. Both men dismounted. "We didn't come that way. We came from Abilene."

Allena frowned. "I didn't know you'd gone to Abilene."

Doug laughed and turned to his friend. "My mother still thinks I'm a little boy who has to ask his mama to come and go."

So this was Mary Lou's elusive brother-in-law. He reminded her of Mac Ludden, the owner of the saloon in Venture, whom Pa called a dandy. Dressed all in black, Doug absently fingered a golden watch fob draped across a fancy satin embroidered vest. He was handsome, but not nearly as comely as Tom or Zack. He resembled Zack, but his jaw hung loosely, separated from the rest of his face by a thin-trimmed mustache underlining a sharp nose and shifty, penetrating eyes that rang alarm signals in Mary Lou.

"Mother," Doug said sweetly and placed a kiss on her forehead. "This is Kenneth Dillard from Boston who's interested in seeing what the wild, wild West looks like."

The dark, handsome stranger with a boyish face tucked the map he carried into his pocket, stepped forward, and with all the suaveness of a gentleman, lifted Allena's fingers to his lips. "My pleasure, madam."

Allena put her arm around Mary Lou. "Doug and Mr. Dillard, this is Mary Lou Langdon—"

"Mary Lou Langdon?" Doug's eyes widened in surprise.

"Yes, Tom's wife."

A smirk crossed Doug's face. He stepped forward quickly, reached for Mary Lou's hand, and captured her gaze. "So my little brother has grown up enough to take himself a wife." He bent his head. His lips brushed and lingered over her fingers, and he tightened his grip as she pulled her hand away. He turned to Kenneth. "My new sister-in-law from—uh—what's the name of your town?"

"Venture, Kansas."

"Oh yes, east of Abilene, I believe."

"No, sir, southwest."

Doug smirked at Kenneth. "Can you imagine my brother keeping her a secret?" He raised his brows and nodded approval. "No wonder he never said a word."

Mr. Dillard bowed over Mary Lou's hand and barely touched it to his lips. "Yes, I can. Mrs. Langdon, my pleasure," he said and stepped back beside Doug.

"Let's get inside out of this heat." Allena took Mr.

Dillard's arm and Doug anchored Mary Lou's hand into the crook of this arm.

"So you're a Kansas girl. You have a sister or two, I hope."

"No, I'm sorry to say."

"So am I." Doug patted her hand.

Mary Lou's stomach churned.

"Where in Boston do you live, Mr. Dillard," Allena asked. "My oldest son, Zack, married a girl from Boston."

"Really? I'll be happy to meet her."

Allena turned to Mary Lou with a knowing glance. "Would you please see if Darcy is able to receive visitors?"

"Darcy?" Mr. Dillard sat up. "Could that be Darcy Whitney? I know a Thomas Whitney family in Boston. Mr. Whitney is a barrister."

Doug laughed. "Wha-da-ya-know."

Allena nodded to Mary Lou. "Tell Darcy that Mr. Kenneth Dillard is here."

Mary Lou knocked on Darcy's door. "Darcy?" No answer. Perhaps she was asleep. Mary Lou quietly opened the door.

Darcy spun from the window. Her face was swollen and red, and her hair hung in disarray. "What do you want?"

"Doug brought a visitor from Boston. He thinks he knows you."

"Boston!" Darcy brightened. "What's his name?" she demanded.

"Kenneth Dillard."

"Kenneth? Kenneth Dillard! I don't believe it." Darcy's face switched from despair to delight. "What on earth could he be doing in this God-forsaken place?" As if on wings, she flew from one wardrobe to another, grabbed dress after dress, draped them over her front, appraised her image in the standing oval mirror, and tossed them on the bed. "None of them fits anymore." Her hands flew to her hair. "Oh, what will I do with my hair?" Finally, she threw a dress on the bed and turned to Mary Lou. "Help me get dressed," she commanded, and opened a bureau drawer for brush and combs.

"No!" Darcy grabbed Mary Lou's arm and shoved her to the door. "Go out and tell Kenneth I'll be there presently, then come back and help me." Darcy opened the door and shoved Mary Lou into the hall.

Mary Lou stood incensed. Darcy was treating her like a maid! Who did she think she was? Mary Lou walked briskly to the main room. *If she thinks I'm coming back, let her dress herself. I'm not going back!*

In the main room, Kenneth Dillard stood holding his lapels, gazing enthralled at the paintings on the wall. "Who painted these?"

"My youngest son, Nelson," Allena said proudly.

"How old is your son?"

"He'll be nineteen in a month."

"So young! He has great feeling for depth and perspective. I'd like to meet that young man if it's possible."

"Of course." Allena looked away from the painting when Mary Lou entered. "Is Darcy coming?"

"Yes. She was resting and will need a little time to make herself presentable. I'm going back to help her." Mary Lou couldn't believe those last words came out of her mouth.

Allena nodded her blessing to Mary Lou. "Mr. Dillard and I are going to Nelson's room to see his paintings." She led the way, chattering as they walked.

"He keeps everything in his bedroom except what hangs on our walls which we change ever so often. His room is on the end corner so he has window lighting from two directions. Nelson will be pleased to meet you. It's a rarity around here to find someone interested in talking about paintings." Allena's voice faded as she and Mr. Dillard walked to the end of the hall into Nelson's room.

On her way back to Darcy, Mary Lou realized she hadn't seen Nelson's roomful of paintings and promised herself to do it in the morning.

Mary Lou knocked and then opened Darcy's door. She was surprised to find that Darcy had completely dressed and was combing her hair with shaking hands. Mary Lou took over. Darcy had wavy hair, soft and fine as silk. *She's beautiful,* Mary Lou thought. *Too bad it's only on the outside.*

Ten minutes later, the young women were on their way back to the main room. Before entering, Darcy paused, patted her hair, pinched her cheeks, pulled herself to fullest height, swept Mary Lou aside, and made a smiling entrance, hands extended. "My dear Kenneth, how delightful. . .to see. . . ."

The room was empty.

Darcy spun to Mary Lou, her face a mask of fury. "What kind of trick. . . ." Her eyes flashed embarrassment and bored holes of hate through Mary Lou.

If Darcy's behavior hadn't been so shocking, Mary Lou would have laughed. But the obvious debilitating effect the vacant room produced also revealed a fresh glimpse of her sister-in-law. Darcy was afraid. In this strange new land, nothing was familiar. The elegant lady she'd been trained to be felt out of place in Texas. Mary Lou had the advantage. Some things were different, but much was familiar. She'd been born a pioneer girl.

Mary Lou's heart begged forgiveness. *I wonder how I'd feel in Boston.* She imagined the raised brows that would greet her appearance in calico. *I'd probably be uncomfortable in Darcy's finery and act like a simpleton and say all the wrong words. Poor Darcy is insecure, homesick, afraid, and going to have her first baby.*

Love tugged open Mary Lou's heart to see the lovely girl who had yet to realize what it meant to be a woman instead of a clothes horse. Was it possible for them to someday be friends in spite of everything? *Lord, I'm going to need lots of help with this one,* Mary Lou prayed.

Nelson's excited chatter and Allena's laughter joined by Mr. Dillard floated up the hall as Darcy and Mary Lou came out of the main room.

Darcy was caught off guard only a second. Her whole demeanor changed. "Kenneth!" she called. "How wonderful to see you." She floated down the hall, a vision of tulle and chiffon, hands outstretched.

four

Mary Lou formed the last loaf of dough, put it in a tin, and covered the eight pans with flannel cloth. Making bread was a satisfying job. She didn't know why; some days the need was an insatiable tyrant.

Mama had always made bread reverently. "It's the staff of life," she used to say. "It shows every Christian his need of Jesus, the Bread of Life for the believer."

Allena had read that verse during their devotion time that morning, as their weekly memory verse. When breakfast was over, Mary Lou and her mother-in-law moved into the main room, read God's Word, discussed the passage, and then finished with prayer for their family, the ranch, their neighbors, and even for the state of Texas. Mary Lou often drew in Kansas and her family back home.

Outside, Hattie passed by the kitchen window, her arms full of dirty clothes. Wash day. She spent a day each week scrubbing smelly barn pants and sweaty shirts for the cowboys. They each gladly paid her a dollar a week.

Mary Lou hurried to the door. "May I help?"

"Nope, this is my job unless you want to carry some water."

Mary Lou hauled buckets and buckets of water until the tubs were full.

Hattie then shooed her away. "Nelson asked about you. Wants you to look at the new picture he painted."

Good. Mary Lou wanted to see it.

Nelson's wheelchair stood outside his door. Mary Lou knocked.

"Come in," Nelson called and greeted her with a wide smile. Other than a low cot and a washstand, the room had no semblance of a bedroom. Canvases and pictures were everywhere, hanging on the walls or stacked against them. No wonder his wheelchair had to stay outside. In a cleared area by the window, Nelson sat on a stool in front of a large easel and canvas, his pencil poised over the sketch he was working on.

"Mind if I visit and watch you paint?"

Nelson grinned broadly. "I hoped you'd come and tell me about the prairie in Kansas. Tom says it's beautiful and would make great paintings."

"It would." Mary Lou's mind formed a picture of their cabin in Kansas surrounded by a broad sweep of ever-swaying prairie grass. "I love the space and openness and the feeling it gives of everything being endless. There's always a breeze blowing. Sometimes it's hot, but it still cools and cleans the air."

"It's like that here," Nelson said.

"Yes, but different. The prairie grass shimmers in the heat, and when the wind blows, the prairie resembles ocean waves rolling in from the sea." Mary Lou laughed. "Tom told me you were tired of painting tumbleweeds."

She turned to profusion of canvases elbowing for space.

She pointed to one. "They might be boring to you, but these tumbleweeds look exactly like the ones I see rolling around the ranch." Mary Lou picked her way, then stooped to a stack leaning against the wall. "Do you mind?" she asked.

Nelson grinned and shook his head.

She thumbed through them and pulled one out. "Nelson, is this Diamond?"

Nelson nodded. "Does it look like him?"

"Look like him! We'd better run and get a saddle or he'll take off without us. Your father would be proud of this. Why isn't it hanging somewhere?"

Nelson rose and grabbed his crutches. In the opposite corner, he brought out canvas after canvas of an imposing man who looked like Zack. "This is my father," he said. His face glowed with pride.

Mary Lou nodded. "He and Zack do look alike."

"But Father was different. He made me feel—whole." Nelson tightened his lip and quickly turned to another stack of pictures, all of his father.

What feeling! It wouldn't have surprised Mary Lou if her father-in-law had spoken. "Your father must have been an extraordinary man."

"He was." Nelson choked up and restacked pictures.

Mary Lou bent to help him. "I know how you feel," she said softly. "I lost my mama." Their eyes met and laid bare the depth of their common suffering.

Nelson returned to his stool.

Mary Lou walked up behind him, hesitated a moment,

then dared to put her arms around him. Here was the sensitive, caring brother she'd always longed for. Her heart raised in praise of God's constant provision for her.

Nelson sat still and didn't move until Mary Lou walked in front of him. He batted tears that moistened his eyes but his mouth was smiling. He ducked his head. "Thank you, Mary Lou."

She spent an hour helping Nelson see Kansas as she had seen it. Suddenly, a thought struck her. "Have you ever thought of selling any of your paintings? I'm sure other people would find them as exciting as I do."

Nelson grinned. "That's what Mr. Dillard said." He shrugged. "But who'd want them? People around here see what I paint all the time. They don't want it hanging on their walls."

"Who knows. Texas people might like what's outside enough to enjoy it on the inside. Maybe the general store in Harness could sell a few. Tom and I plan to go back to Kansas for a visit next year. We could take a few and put them in Father's store and even take some to Abilene. There are lots of people there. How do you know if you don't try?"

A new light twinkled in Nelson's eyes, a new purpose took root.

Mary Lou left him enthusiastically back at work on his sketch. She felt restless so she walked to the corral. Dulcie nodded her head, tossing a welcome with her mane.

"Good morning, friend. How would you like to ride?"

Dulcie whinnied and pranced. Mary Lou looked toward

the barn. Tom knelt on the roof, hammering. Ladders leaned against the sides, and two cowboys climbed up and down like agile prairie dogs, carrying boards. She waved at Tom.

He wiped his face on his sleeve, waved, and immediately went back to work. Mary Lou had her answer. He was too busy to ride.

Dulcie whinnied and pranced.

"Sorry, dear girl, but you know the rules. Women do not ride alone in Texas. Between the Mexicans, Indians, and animals, Tom says it's too dangerous." Mary Lou rubbed Dulcie's face and soft nose. "Now if we were back in Kansas—"

"Mary Lou!"

Mary Lou turned toward the call.

Allena stood on the porch and motioned her back to the house.

As Mary Lou neared she saw Allena's troubled face.

"Have you seen Darcy this morning?"

Mary Lou shook her head. "I was with Nelson. Why?"

"I can't find her." Allena pursed her lips and shook her head. "I thought she was in her room, but she's not."

"She has to be here somewhere," Mary Lou said reassuringly. "Don't worry, we'll find her."

They didn't. By the time they'd searched the house and surrounding area, it was obvious Darcy had disappeared.

"Maybe she went with Zack to town this morning," Mary Lou suggested.

"Surely they would have told me." In sudden anguish,

Allena looked toward the corral. "Do you think that silly girl. . .?" She ran toward the stables and hailed Tex.

Tex nodded. "Yes, ma'am." She came this morning and told me to saddle her up a horse. I wondered but. . . ." Tex shrugged his shoulders.

Allena paled. "When? What time?

"About nine."

Allena swung toward the barn, headed for the tack room, and told Tex to get their horses. Halfway there, she stopped and shaded her eyes. A horse galloped hard across the field.

"The saddle's empty!" Mary Lou cried.

Allena called Tex and pointed. "Is that the horse you saddled for Miss Darcy?"

Tex squinted and nodded. "Yes, ma'am, that's the one."

Allena ran to the barn and told Tom. The three men scrambled down from the roof, saddled, and galloped off. Tex joined them.

Allena watched them go, shaking her head. "That girl knew she shouldn't ride alone. She's been told often enough. Sometimes I wonder what kind of upbringing she had. She does anything she pleases when Zack isn't here!"

Allena's sharp voice surprised Mary Lou. It was the first time she'd seen her mother-in-law angry. Allena had cried out in anger, but her face was pained in anguish. Whatever possessed Darcy to do such a foolish thing? And with child! Come to think of it, nothing had been said at dinner last night. Allena, Hattie, and Mary Lou had agreed to say nothing of their discovery until Darcy had told Zack.

Surely if Zack had known, he'd have announced it at supper. Could it be that Darcy hadn't told him and had ridden out with the intention of. . .?

No. She wouldn't! Yet yesterday, Darcy had been so emphatic about not wanting. . . . Mary Lou shook her head. Her gaze connected with Allena's. Were Allena's thoughts mirrors of her own? Would Darcy do something dangerous in hopes that the horse might slip, fall or. . . .No. She wouldn't think that of Darcy.

As soon as the men left, Allena busied with preparations to care for Darcy when she came home.

Hattie got a tub of boiling water ready. It seemed Hattie got a tub of boiling water ready for everything.

Suddenly, Allena grabbed Hattie and Mary Lou's arms. "We must pray," she said.

The three women sank to their knees in silence, heads bowed.

Softly, Allena began to pray aloud. "Father, my child is out there alone. . . ."

Mary Lou opened her eyes and looked up at Allena. My child. Regardless of how Darcy acted, Allena accepted her as her child. Humbled, Mary Lou asked God's forgiveness for the thoughts she harbored of a spoiled, selfish, rude girl who seemed to consider no one but herself.

Allena's voice faded back in. "But she doesn't know You yet, Lord. Give us time to love her enough so she feels it, and recognizes she is hurting herself more than anyone else. Oh God, keep her safe. Forgive me for my selfishness in thinking only of the baby she carries. Let no harm come to either of them. Thank You, Father. In Jesus' name, Amen."

After a momentary pause, Hattie nodded. "Thy will be done."

The morning dragged on interminably. No one could concentrate. Finally, Allena took a stool and sat on the shady side of the house facing the direction the men left, furiously knitting a sock. Mary Lou sat beside her, checked clothes, mended, and sewed buttons where they were missing. Hattie rattled around in the kitchen, coming out periodically to peer, hand over eyes, into the distance.

Nelson joined their vigil. Mary Lou brought out the painting he was working on.

No one said much, but Mary Lou felt surrounded by ascending prayer. Foolish, foolish girl, her mind repeated. But hadn't she had the same idea that morning? She'd yearned to saddle Dulcie and ride out into the wide spaces that stretched before her to enjoy the exhilarating feeling of flying with the wind. Mary Lou thanked God she hadn't.

Or had God given her the idea to ride? Like the morning of her wedding, when the urge to ride sent her to the cottonwoods and Tom was there. He had said he'd felt compelled to ride there, too. She'd been awed at what he said. "Now I know God answers prayers." Had this been God's guiding? Maybe if Mary Lou had satisfied her yearning this morning, she'd have sighted Darcy or found her.

No. Mama had always said that two wrongs never made a right. In the area in Kansas where Mary Lou had grown up, it had been comparatively safe to ride alone, but she seldom had. Her father, mother, Jenny, Aunt Nelda, or Glenn usually had accompanied her.

Here in Texas, only the bravest rode alone. Even though it seemed peaceful, marauders, without warning, regularly descended to raid and plunder. No, she had to believe she'd done the right thing. Anyway, God had Darcy in His hands whether she accepted Him as Lord or not. What was the verse Mama always repeated? "We love Him because He first loved us" (1 John 4:19). Yes, God loved Darcy.

Mary Lou closed her eyes. *Keep her safe, Father. Let no harm come to the baby. You know if Allena lost her first grandchild, it would break her heart. You know what it is to lose a son. . . .*

"Here they come!" Nelson shouted. He dropped his pencil, tucked his crutches under his arms, and moved amazingly fast across the yard.

Everyone followed and ran toward the cloud of dust and horses. Had they found her?

Tom had Darcy in his arms. Allena and Hattie caught her as Tom slid her off the saddle.

Darcy, her face smudged with dirt, was pale and semiconscious. She whimpered, opened her eyes, slid her arms around Allena's neck, and sighed.

Tom dismounted and carried Darcy to her bedroom.

She opened her eyes and stared up at Tom. "Oh, Tom, I love you," she said, fainting in his arms.

Mary Lou's heart stopped. *I love you?* She immediately chided herself. She loved him as a brother, of course. It was

Darcy's way of saying thank you. She was shaken and didn't know what she was saying.

Allena shooed everyone out of the bedroom except Hattie. "This bedroom won't hold us all. Hattie and I will find out if she's hurt and let you know."

Mary Lou felt a tinge of rejection, but as Mama always had declared, sometimes too many are no help at all. She went to find Tom.

At the barn, he stood unsaddling Tinder.

"Where did you find her?"

"About three miles south of the bog. We saw horse tracks go around the bog, so we followed them to the top of the knoll. They stopped there, then turned and went back. We found Darcy at the bottom. She either fell from her horse or the horse slipped and threw her and she rolled down. She was scared, moaning, and crying when we found her. I don't think she's hurt. She rode home in no noticeable pain."

Mary Lou shook her head. "I hope it didn't hurt the baby."

Tom swung and stared with his mouth open. "What baby?"

Mary Lou could have bitten her tongue. Now she had to tell Tom. "Yesterday, we found Darcy sick, and Mother suspects she's with child. But don't say anything yet. We don't know whether Zack knows and Darcy should be the one to tell him."

Tom nodded. He turned back to Tinder and methodically slid off the saddle, swung it over the side of the stall, removed the saddle blanket, and absently rubbed Tinder's back. Without looking at her, he said, "Mary Lou, will you promise me something?"

"Anything, Tom."

"When you're with child, will you please tell me first?"

Mary Lou smiled and slid between Tom and Tinder. Their eyes met and held. "Mr. Langdon, you'll be the first to know." His arms encircled her, and he drew her close and kissed her tenderly. Arms around each other, they walked outside.

The men had already climbed back on the roof. Tom went up the ladder and joined them.

Mary Lou paced back and forth in front of Darcy's bedroom door. Periodically, Darcy cried out and moaned. Allena and Hattie's voices were muted, so Mary Lou heard little.

Finally the door opened and Hattie came out.

"Is she all right?" Mary Lou asked.

"Don't seem to be hurt much, no bones broken, just scrapes, bumps, and bruises. That's all we can see."

"The baby?"

Hattie shrugged her shoulders. "Allena's been listening to see if she can hear anything."

If that baby dies, part of Allena will die with it. Dear Jesus, please. . . .

Mary Lou, to calm her fears, joined Hattie in the kitchen to help with dinner. Tom came in and said he'd sent Tex to Harness for Zack.

When Allena entered the kitchen, her brows were knit

with worry. "Mary Lou, would you sit with Darcy, please? I think she's asleep."

Mary Lou tiptoed into the bedroom, quietly pulled up a chair, and sat down. Darcy's face was relaxed from her usual expression of antagonism. Even with bruises and scratches, she looked beautiful. Her luxurious chestnut hair trailed across the pillow, highlighting flushed cheeks that cupped like soft rose petals on a fragile doll.

The door opened quietly. Tom peeked in, entered slowly, and stooped beside Mary Lou's chair. "She all right?" he whispered.

Mary Lou nodded. "Your mother says she couldn't find anything wrong except scrapes and bruises."

Darcy stirred and opened her eyes. "Tom?"

Tom patted Darcy's hand. "You're home, Darcy. Everything's going to be all right."

"Thank you," she said weakly. "I prayed you'd come."

Darcy had prayed Tom would come? Maybe there was hope for her yet. Then a disturbing thought gnawed at Mary Lou: Why hadn't Darcy prayed for Zack?

Tom patted Darcy's hand, kissed Mary Lou on the cheek, mouthed good-bye, and left quietly.

When Mary Lou turned back to Darcy, the young woman was staring at her.

"I'm glad you're safe and not hurt, Darcy. We were all very worried about you."

"You were?" A strange look crossed Darcy's face and relaxed into a smile.

Mary Lou patted Darcy's hand. "Yes, and we hoped

nothing would happen to the baby."

Darcy withdrew her hand immediately. Her sweet smile dissolved into her usual petulant expression. "Of course," she stated flatly. "Nothing must happen to the baby." She turned and squeezed away tears that flooded her long lashes. "Not Allena's first grandchild!"

Mary Lou saw the tears and immediately regretted her reference to the baby. Her heart sank. She'd lost her. For a moment, Darcy had opened up an opportunity to talk, but Mary Lou had spoiled it. Could it be Darcy felt no one liked her, or that she was miserably homesick? How terrible that would be. Once again, Mary Lou vowed to try and befriend the beautiful, lonesome, unhappy girl.

five

Victor's hooves pounded a dust storm. Zack leaned as he rode through the Circle Z arch to the ranch house, dropped to the ground, and ran through the front door, wild-eyed and breathless. "Where is she?"

Allena motioned with her hand. "She's—"

He brushed past his mother and Mary Lou, who both hurried down the hall behind him.

"Zack! She's all right. Shook up and bruised a bit, but not hurt."

He opened the bedroom door, rushed in, sat on the side of the bed, and reached for Darcy's hand. "Darling, it's me. Are you all right? Do you hurt anywhere?" He gently gathered her into his arms.

Darcy moaned, opened her eyes, let out a cry, and circled her arms tightly around Zack's neck.

Zack stroked her hair and cradled her like a baby. "It's all right. Doctor Mike will be here shortly." Darcy's eyes widened. "Doctor? I don't need a doctor." She sat up, anxiety dancing from one blue eye to the other.

"I didn't know how bad you were hurt or whether you'd broken any bones. I wasn't taking any chances, darling."

"But. . .," Darcy sputtered.

Tom came in, followed by Dr. Mike. The doctor moved briskly to his patient's side, took her hand, and fingered her pulse.

Zack stood and stepped back.

Dr. Mike smiled. "Well, young lady, I see you haven't been in Texas long enough to know you're supposed to stay on the back of the horse to ride." He laughed at his little joke.

No one else did.

He turned to the worried faces surrounding him and shooed them toward the door. "You can be sure I'll take good care of my patient. Wait outside, please."

Zack moved to the foot of the bed.

Holding Darcy's limp wrist, Dr. Mike stared at Zack. "That means you, too."

Zack hesitated, casting a despairing look at Darcy.

Dr. Mike straightened up and turned a beady eye on Zack. "And close the door behind you."

Zack left.

Everyone stood in the hall and leaned against its walls.

"We could all have coffee," Allena suggested.

Heads shook no.

Zack's gaze searched his family. "How did it happen?"

No one replied.

Zack straightened. "Is something wrong? Somebody say something!"

Allena spoke. "Darcy was out riding—"

"Who with?"

"She went out alone."

"Alone!" Zack's eyes blazed. "Who saddled her horse?"

"Tex."

Zack swung and started down the hall.

Tom jumped and grabbed his arm. "Whoa! You can't blame Tex. Darcy has a way of getting…." Tom hesitated, obviously uncomfortable.

"Getting her own way." Zack finished. "Nobody knows that better than I do. But why didn't somebody stop her?"

Allena moved to Zack's side and placed a steadying hand on his shoulder. "None of us knew she was gone. No one saw her come downstairs. Around lunch time we missed her. Mary Lou and I looked everywhere. We finally asked Tex if he'd seen her. He said she had insisted he saddle her a horse. We were just about saddled up to ride out and find her when Buttons came home empty. So Tom, Tex, and Bart rode out and followed the trail."

Tom picked up the story. "That good rain we had last night marked us a clear trail to Bog Hollow. The tracks walked along the edge, danced around, turned, and headed back home. We figured something must have spooked or tripped the horse and knocked Darcy off. We followed marks where she rolled down to the edge of the bog. Thank God a log stopped her and kept her from rolling into the mire. That's where we found her, lying against the log in tears, afraid to move. When I carried her home on Tinder, she didn't seem hurt."

The bedroom door opened. Dr. Mike came out smiling and shook Zack's hand.

Everyone came to attention.

"Your wife is fine. A few bumps and scrapes, but no broken bones. And I don't think the baby is harmed."

Zack's eyes widened and his mouth fell open. "Baby? What baby?"

"You didn't know? Your wife's about three months in the family way."

For the first time in his life, Zack was speechless.

Dr. Mike grinned, grabbed Zack's hand again, and pumped it briskly. "Congratulations! Hope it's a fine boy to carry on the Langdon name."

Surprised shock dissolved into relief. A silly grin spread across Zack's face and turned on a twinkle in his eyes. "Well, wha-da-ya-know!" Zack's glazed gaze moved from one family member to another. "I'm going to be a father!" he shouted and bolted through the bedroom door.

His family's happy smiles were tinged with guilt. Zack had been the last to know.

Hattie appeared at the end of the hall. "Mrs. Langdon, dinner's ready."

"Thank you, Hattie." Allena turned to Dr. Mike. "Won't you join us before you go? You have to eat. Might as well fill up at our table with us."

Dr. Mike joyfully accepted, settled himself before a heaping plate of steak, potatoes, and vegetables, and monopolized the conversation between mouthfuls, catching everyone up on the comings and goings of his territory.

"The Peabodys down at the old Wilson place are leaving. Henry never was cut out for ranching in the first place. He never liked taking care of animals—said he'd rather hunt and eat them." The doctor shoveled a mound of potatoes into his mouth. "If truth were known, I think he's afraid of them." He laughed. "Without his spunky little wife, Agatha, and their boys, Fred and George, Peabody would never have lasted this long."

Doc accepted another helping of steak and potatoes. "Too bad. Nice family. Hate to lose them. I guess Henry and Agatha are going back East but the boys want to stay here and hire on as cowboys. All they have to do is talk their mother into it. Fred is sixteen and George is fourteen, good training age."

Allena looked at Tom. "Think we could use a couple more? I like Agatha. She's a strong, godly woman and raised those boys right. I think she'd feel better if they were settled into a job with some neighbors she knew."

Tom glanced at Zack, who nodded. "If you see them, Doc, tell them to come around," Zack said.

"I'll do that." Dr. Mike finished off his second piece of Hattie's shoofly pie and rose, patting his stomach and bowing to Allena. "Madam, it's a rare treat to have the chance to enjoy dinner with such lovely ladies."

Hattie entered with another piece of pie.

Dr. Mike held up his hand and bowed to her. "Madam, you do me honor, but my stomach objects. I compliment you. It's the best shoofly pie I've eaten, bar none."

Hattie nodded, shyly smiled, and carried the pie back to the kitchen.

"Well, I must be on my way. I suppose somebody's out trying to find me," Dr. Mike said.

Everyone stood. The men walked out with Dr. Mike.

Darcy rose, hurried to Zack, grabbed his hand, and marched out alongside him, head held high.

Silence hung heavy.

Allena looked at Nelson and Mary Lou. "Let's forget we knew and congratulate Zack as if we just heard the news."

Both nodded, and Mary Lou renewed within her promise that she would tell Tom first when the time came.

Allena returned to the table and beckoned Hattie in to clear it.

"I must say I'm concerned about Darcy. The way she

smothers Zack is unnatural."

Mary Lou poured them each a cup of coffee and sat down beside Allena. "Maybe she's feels...uh...that he's the only one who loves her."

Allena's raised brows asked a question.

Mary Lou went on. "I think she feels the family hasn't accepted her."

"That's not true. I've accepted her, but she pushes me away. I know part of it is she doesn't want to be here. She's unhappy that Zack refused her father and came back home to set up his law practice. Her heart and mind are still in Boston. She misses the social life.

"Life is so different here. Before you came, we attended Betsy Travis's wedding at the ranch east of us. I'm afraid Darcy looked more like the bride than the bride. She made people uncomfortable, and she was miserable. I've tried to treat her same as I'd treat my own daughter if I had one, but she doesn't make it easy." Allena thoughtfully sipped her coffee. "I love her because Zack loves her. He sees a loveliness in her we haven't found yet."

"Mama always said there's good in everyone, but sometimes we have to look awfully hard to find it." Mary Lou studied Allena for a moment. Dare she be honest? She decided to chance it. "When I sat with Darcy after her accident and told her we were all worried about her, she seemed surprised and pleased. Then I mentioned we were grateful nothing happened to the baby and she drew back into herself again. I wonder if she feels we're only concerned about the baby, not her."

Allena sat staring into her coffee cup.

Mary Lou continued. "You think maybe she feels all

alone with Zack gone so much? I know I miss Tom when the work keeps him going twelve hours a day."

"Could be," Allena mused. "I've asked Darcy to do things with me, but she refuses and bluntly comments that at home, they have servants to take care of such things."

Mary Lou laughed and confessed to bristling at some of Darcy's caustic remarks. "I was thinking, it's easier for me than Darcy. Much that I do here is similar to what I've always done back home. From her comments, she's led a pampered life. It's not her fault her family lived in a big house with servants. She's been deprived of the chance to learn what we pioneer girls take for granted." Mary Lou paused to catch and assemble the jumble of thoughts tumbling in her head. "I wonder."

"Wonder? About what?"

"How I can pull Darcy into the family. I'm her age. I'm new in the family. I didn't know what a daughter-in-law was supposed to do until I asked Hattie if I could make bread." Mary Lou's new thoughts intrigued her. She faced Allena. "Mother, do you suppose I could teach Darcy to make bread?"

Allena suppressed a smile and nodded. "All you can do is try. You have my blessing."

Mary Lou began the next morning, after devotions. Darcy, as usual, left the breakfast table with Zack and walked with him to the barn to get Victor and wave him off. Most of the time, she returned to her room. Sometimes though, she walked to the wooden bench under the mesquite trees and sat and stared into the distance. This morning, Mary Lou watched her slowly walk into the house and return to her room.

Mary Lou waited for a while, then knocked on Darcy's door. "Who is it?"

"Mary Lou."

No answer.

Mary Lou was about to turn away when the door slowly opened. Darcy's blank face perused her sister-in-law. "What do you want?"

"I just wondered how you felt this morning."

Darcy eyed her with suspicion. "I'm all right, considering."

If I don't step in now, the door will be closed tighter the next time, Mary Lou thought. "Since we're both newcomers to this family, we ought to find time and make the effort to get to know each other better."

Darcy raised her eyebrows. "Why this sudden friendly interest?"

"Well, I'm the newest one, and at first felt I should wait until others approached me. But when they don't. . . ." Mary Lou shrugged.

For a questioning moment Darcy stared at her. Suddenly a charming smile broke her mask. She swung the door open. "Come in," she said and stepped back.

Mary Lou had been told that when Zack came home, Allena moved into one of the smaller bedrooms and gave the master bedroom with the fireplace to the newlyweds. The room was twice the size of Tom's. Two large wardrobes almost filled one wall, and a four poster bed projected into the center of the room on a multi-colored rug. Behind the door, a large wash stand with a china basin and pitcher sat under an oval mirror hung on the wall. This lovely bedroom surely was equivalent to what Darcy had back East. Aunt Tibby's home had been one of the grandest in Venture, but this room was larger than any in the Bar-B ranch. Mary Lou would be grateful for such a room.

At the moment, though, it wasn't too neat. The bed, still unmade, held several of Darcy's dresses, one draped dejectedly over the tall foot rail. Two others were thrown on a chair.

Darcy's gaze followed Mary Lou's to the strewn clothing. "I'm used to having a maid," she said bluntly, then gathered the dresses from the chair into one arm and opened the wardrobe with the other to expose dress after dress of delicate fabrics and colors, mostly blue.

"Blue must be your favorite color," Mary Lou said.

"It goes with my eyes."

Mary Lou ran her hand over the soft cloth of the pale blue and cream sateen dress draped over the bottom of the bed. "This is lovely."

"You can have it." Darcy grimaced. "It's too small for me. Since I'm carrying this baby, I don't fit anything. Mrs. Cassidy will have to make me something. Maybe she can make me some baggy clothes, since she can't make anything to fit."

"You always look lovely, even in Mrs. Cassidy's clothes."

Darcy dipped her head and narrowed her eyes. "Was there something special you wanted this morning?"

Maybe Mary Lou had stayed too long. "Like I said, I'd like us to be friends as well as sisters-in-law."

"All right." Suddenly Darcy dropped her guard. Sad eyes betrayed her unhappiness. "I could use a friend."

After that visit, it seemed Darcy looked forward to Mary

Lou's morning chats, although Mary Lou never knew exactly what reception she'd receive.

One day they began talking about their childhood homes. Darcy radiated as she described the fancy balls, horse racing, family vacations at the ocean, and the young ladies' finishing school she'd attended in Boston to learn the etiquette and social manners needed to be the mistress of a large house with servants.

"We could have had all that if Zack would have joined my father's law firm." Her voice dripped bitterness.

"Texas needs good lawyers, too."

"Exactly what Zack said." Darcy lowered her head. "When I agreed to marry him and come here, I never realized it would be so primitive." Darcy raised wistful eyes. "I wish you could see how lovely my home is in Boston. It's brick with trees all around and paths one can walk on with pretty shoes." Suddenly, Darcy's face relaxed into a totally unguarded expression and she swung toward her wardrobe. "Here," she said. "Try this on."

Amid giggles, Darcy unbuttoned Mary Lou's skirt and it dropped to the floor with her shirtwaist. She threw two crisp petticoats over Mary Lou's head and pinned them tightly around her waist.

"At least you have a tiny waist," Darcy commented and swung a shimmering blue moire ball gown over Mary Lou's head. She unbraided Mary Lou's long hair, describing the elaborate coiffures and styles in Boston, then swept the wealth of chestnut tresses to form a twist loosely wrapped around Mary Lou's head, deftly anchored with shell combs and a plume feather.

Darcy's whole countenance and demeanor changed to

charming enthusiasm. She draped a golden necklace around Mary Lou's throat and handed her a pair of cream high-button shoes.

Donning long white gloves, Mary Lou stood staring into the mirror at a woman she'd never seen before. She felt like an elegant lady. No wonder Darcy liked to dress in these clothes. Suddenly she was struck with how much she looked like Mama in a picture taken when she was a teacher in Toledo before she married Pa. Mary Lou giggled and wished Tom could see her in this finery.

Mary Lou noticed the expression on Darcy's face was completely new; the petulance, gone. The face reflected beside Mary Lou's in the mirror radiated and glowed with warmth. This must be the girl Zack saw. No wonder he loved her.

The two girls were still absorbed in their finery when the ranch bell pealed from Hattie's impatient hand.

"Oh, my goodness," Mary Lou cried, "I didn't do my job of setting the table!"

Darcy helped her out of her finery and Mary Lou slipped into her calico dress.

They hurried to the dining room. Everyone was seated. The two girls slipped into their places, smiling faces veiled with mystery.

Allena's questioning gaze traveled from one to the other and then turned to Tom. "Say grace, please."

The next morning, Mary Lou knocked on Darcy's door carrying one of her calico dresses. "I brought this dress because I didn't think you'd want to learn to bake bread in any of your lovely ones."

"Bake bread! I've never baked bread in my life, nor do

I intend to."

For a moment Darcy's indignant stare dampened Mary Lou's resolve. "Oh, but it's fun and such a satisfying job. I think you'll enjoy it."

"That's a servant's job." Darcy's stare turned to outrage. "Ladies don't—"

"Yesterday you said I looked like a lady. Today am I a servant just because I have on a calico dress and make bread?"

Darcy lifted her nose in the air and closed the door.

That bedroom is Darcy's escape, Mary Lou thought. *It must be pretty lonesome to primp and read your time away.* Mary Lou knocked again and waited. Just as she turned to leave, the door opened.

The two girls gazed at each other.

Mary Lou felt Darcy's searching distrust, yet a yearning bled through her indignant mask. "You don't have to do anything," Mary Lou coaxed. "I thought you might watch while I made bread and see if you'd like to try." For a moment Mary Lou thought Darcy was going to step back and slam the door in her face.

Darcy cast a glance at the calico dress, then lifted her nose "I'll come, but I won't wear that!"

Mary Lou felt she'd won a small opening as they walked together to the kitchen.

When they entered, Hattie looked up in surprise, but wise old bird that she was, she gave a disinterested nod and continued measuring flour for bread.

"Darcy and I are going to make bread."

Hattie's hand halted midair, poised to empty a cup of flour. It obviously took great control for her to keep her mouth shut. She bobbed her head, put the cup down, dusted the flour from her hands, and wiped them on her apron. "Good." It came out in a squeak. She cleared her throat. "Can use all the loaves you girls want to make." She hurried outside to her wash tubs.

Darcy didn't touch a thing, but she watched Mary Lou expertly check the bread recipe she didn't need, combine the flour, yeast, sugar, salt, water, and milk, beat and punch the dough, and form it into loaves.

Darcy gingerly held the bread pans while Mary Lou placed the loaves in them.

"Now, then. You can surprise Zack and tell him you and I made bread today."

Darcy's expression was, as usual, unfathomable. What went on behind those beautiful clouded eyes? She was like a wild, changeable wind: gentle, soothing, and pleasant one moment, and then an unpredictable, gathering storm the next.

Thank You, Lord. We've taken the first step.

six

Morning chores done, Mary Lou strolled to the corral and clapped her hands.

Dulcie, ears alert, whinnied, tossed her head, and came on a run.

"How about a little workout in the corral?" Mary Lou patted Dulcie's warm sleek neck and opened the gate.

Dulcie nuzzled Mary Lou's shoulder and danced behind her mistress.

Mary Lou swung the double barn doors wide and walked to Dulcie's stall, her frisky horse at her heels. She adjusted the bridle, smoothed Dulcie's blanket over her back, swung the saddle into place, pulled the girth, and tightened the cinch. Just like home. A hot breeze blew through the barn accentuating strong straw and animal odors that gnawed strangely at Mary Lou's stomach.

In the corral, Mary Lou settled in the saddle and rode the fence line, relishing the movement. Other than when she and Tom rode in the cool of the evening, her riding had been curbed, much to her dislike. The warmth and bouncing produced a new unpleasant feeling. Her stomach grew queasy, her head felt light. She glanced up at a sun suddenly grown hot. In defense, she turned Dulcie back toward the barn, much to her horse's displeasure. It was worse inside. Pungent odors perched Mary Lou's stomach on a precarious edge. She hurriedly unsaddled Dulcie, slapped her backside, and sent her reluctantly back into the corral. Slowly, shakily, Mary Lou walked back to the house.

The kitchen felt blessedly cool. Hattie, surrounded by pie making, looked up and smiled a welcome.

Mary Lou took a deep breath. "Need some help?"

"Bread's gettin' low," Hattie answered.

Immediately, Mary Lou set about gathering bread pans, flour, and mixing bowls and took them to the table. Up to her elbows in bread dough, Mary Lou found the aroma of the bread suddenly intolerable. Without warning, her stomach flipped and she felt clammy. Her eyes refused to focus. The walls swayed! She grabbed the edge of the table.

"Hattie, I feel terrible. Can you finish this bread?"

At her side at once, Hattie guided her to the wash basin, rinsed her hands, and then applied a cold wet cloth to her forehead. "You been lookin' mighty peaked lately." Hattie's mouth arched into a wry smile. "Miss Mary, have you missed your monthly?"

Mary Lou's mind rolled over the months. She looked sheepishly at Hattie, then shivered. A delicious shiver! She dried her hands quickly and set out to find Tom. Jess, the only one around, told her Tom and some of the boys had ridden over to see Will Shepard.

Disappointed, Mary Lou returned to her bedroom and busied herself picking over her dresses. Most of them were fitted at the waist. She smiled, trying to picture herself with a full stomach. Her first baby! What would they name him? Thomas, of course. Thomas Owen? After her father? *Oh Lord, would a grandson give Pa the will to live?*

Or—delightful thought—it could be a girl. Sweet times she and Mama had shared flooded Mary Lou's mind, and tears welled up in her eyes. Then, she remembered. All Stafford girls carried the name Elizabeth. Her daughter must continue the line. Grandmother Stafford had been Ruthella Elizabeth, Mama had been Ellen Lisbeth, Aunt Tibby was Elizabeth Mae, she was Mary Lou Elizabeth. Which sounded better, Ellen Lizabeth—or—Lizbeth Ellen. Either way they would call her Beth. Mary Lou imagined her mother gathering a little namesake girl into her loving arms and her eyes grew moist.

Joy and anticipation flooded Mary Lou's heart to near bursting. She sighed deeply, laid both hands on her stomach, and raised her eyes. *Thank You, Father, my cup runneth over.*

She sat inside and mended. The morning dragged. Intermittent buoyancy and excitement gave way to nagging nausea. She paused often, listening for the pound of Tinder's hoofbeats, longing for Tom to come. She tried to imagine what he would say. They had not talked much about children.

The dinner bell bonged under Hattie's persistent hand. When all gathered, there was only Allena, Darcy, and Mary Lou. Doug and Zack were in Harness. If the work at Shepards were unfinished, Tom would eat with them.

Mary Lou squirmed to find a comfortable spot on her chair. She stared at food which held no appeal. The smell of it played havoc with her stomach. She smiled at Allena. "I'm not very hungry, Mother, just tired. If you don't mind, I think I'll go rest for a little while."

Allena's brows squinted a question, but her mouth

remained closed—for which Mary Lou was thankful. She feared she would not be able to keep the news from her mother-in-law if Allena asked. Above all, Mary Lou wanted to keep her promise to Tom that he would be the first to know. As for Hattie, nothing that happened in the Langdon household ever escaped that shrewd, old woman, yet her loyalty to each member kept her silent.

It seemed she had just closed her eyes when the bedroom door creaked and Tom stood at the bedside. His suntanned face, creased with worry, stared at her. "You all right? Mother said—"

"I'm fine." Mary Lou smiled. What a perfect time and place to tell him.

"Mother said you were out riding, came in not feeling well, and didn't eat dinner. For November, the sun's unusually hot today." Tom's eyes clouded with concern.

Mary Lou tingled with excitement. *It's unkind to worry him, but I want this to be a special moment. Our first child!*

She nodded. "The sun was hot, and for the first time I didn't enjoy riding Dulcie. The bouncing, the barn odors were too much for me because. . . ." She stood up, circled her arms around Tom's neck, and looked into the depths of his eyes. "Because we're going to have a baby."

Tom's eyes registered shock and surprise. Then a timid smile slowly crinkled the corners of his mouth and raced across his astonished face.

It was what she had been waiting to see.

Tom's arms circled her. He kissed her eyes, her cheeks, drank in the joy radiating in her upturned face, then captured her lips.

Mary Lou sensed a new oneness between them that she

had never felt before.

"Wha-da-ya-know!" he drawled. "My big brother isn't as far ahead of me as he thinks he is!" Tom straightened up. Mary Lou's feet left the floor and he swung her around, kissing her cheeks, her eyes, her mouth. Suddenly he stopped and eased Mary Lou to the floor. Tom's gaze, suddenly serious, quizzed hers. "Am I the first to know?" His voice was husky.

"You are the first to know," Mary Lou assured him. "Except Hattie."

Tom's face fell.

Mary Lou cupped his face in her hands. "It was Hattie who told me! I almost fainted on her this morning while making bread, and she guessed right away. I went to find you and you were gone." She watched his smile return and she stretched to reach his lips for a tender, lingering kiss.

Mary Lou settled into her husband's arms. His kisses on her mouth and cheek, his whispered love into her hair, carried warm caressing joy to every part of her body. God had joined a special part of each of them and in eight or so months would give them the gift of a child. She sighed contentedly. "I hope it's a boy and looks just like you."

"Or a beautiful little girl, like you." Suddenly, Tom released Mary Lou and grabbed her hand. "Come on, woman, let's shout it to the world." He reached the door, stopped abruptly, and shook his head. "Nope. We'll calmly announce it at supper."

Much to Mary Lou's surprise, Tom waited until halfway through supper before he stood, grinned, and tapped his spoon on his cup. "I bring great news," he began.

All heads turned.

"It gives me great pleasure to announce that the Thomas Langdon family is on the increase." His eyes twinkled.

It took a minute for the family to comprehend what he had said. Allena caught it first. She rose smiling, moved quickly around the table, and threw her arms about Tom. Then she turned and pulled Mary Lou to her feet, hugging and kissing her. She embraced her son again. "Wonderful! Now there will be two arrows in my quiver."

Darcy sat silently toying with her food, her stone face an enigma. At Allena's comment, she raised her chin and swept a haughty gaze around the table. "It looks like we're going to have a race to see who becomes the heir of the Langdon estate." She returned her gaze to her plate and placed a forkful of food in her mouth.

Silence hovered over the table, faces stunned.

An embarrassed red curtain lowered over Zack's countenance. He stared at Darcy for a moment, his face stern. "There's no race for the Langdon estate as you call it. This ranch belongs to all of us."

Darcy tossed her head. "Well, Doug is making sure he gets his share and then some."

Zack's fierce gaze pinned his wife. "That's between me, Doug, Tom, Nelson, and Mother. We'll discuss it no more, especially at the supper table." He surveyed the immobile faces of his family. "Does everyone understand that?"

Without hesitation, Tom answered, "Yes, Zack, and I agree with you."

Mary Lou's stomach churned, but not because of the baby. Why did Darcy say such things and embarrass Zack? It happened time and time again. Was she that afraid she was going to be cheated? By her own family? What kind of a family did she have in Boston that fostered such suspicion?

Darcy rose indignantly and flounced out. Silence again filled the room, broken by heaving sighs.

Zack sat with his head down, the muscles of his jaws flexing. Abruptly, he looked up. "I ask forgiveness for my wife," he said in a low voice. "She's homesick and says things without thinking."

Mary Lou remembered one of Nelson's pictures of their father. He looked exactly as Zack did now. Stern but compassionate. It must be hard for Zack to follow in his father's footsteps without the support of a strong, loving wife. Father Langdon had Allena at his side. Allena would never have said a thing like that. Mary Lou glanced at her mother-in-law. Allena's eyes reflected deep hurt—not for herself, but for the burden carried by her oldest son.

Allena picked up her fork. "Let's eat our supper. It's getting cold." She turned toward the kitchen door. "Hattie, I think we need another pitcher of milk."

Hattie appeared immediately with a pitcher and removed the empty one. The table was soon empty, and Hattie cleared the dishes.

Early fall and winter suddenly filled the days with endless work. Harvesting and preparing enough food to feed and sustain all the people and animals on the Circle Z until spring was a momentous task.

Tom and the cowboys killed cows and hogs, hunted antelope and buffalo, butchered, and scraped, cleaned, and hung skins in the barn to dry.

The women spent endless days preserving meat: cutting strips to dry for jerky, packing some of the best parts in the snow to freeze, grinding sausage, salting and smoking hams and bacon, submerging pork and beef in barrels of congealed fat, and lining the barrels against the outer wall in the cold shed adjoining the kitchen. As the barrels emptied, the women rendered and clarified the fat into lard.

Darcy threw her hands up in horror and retreated to other parts of the house, but then she surprised everyone by setting the dining room table for dinner one noon.

Like a spry old mouse, Hattie, on all fours, her apron pinned into a pouch filled with vegetables, climbed up and down a ladder into the cool root cellar dug under part of the kitchen and sorted her bounty into bins and crates.

Mary Lou and Allena filled flour sacks with nuts, dried beans, potatoes, onions, and a variety of squash and handed them down to Hattie.

Even Darcy wandered into the kitchen one day and sorted vegetables, only to complain later that her hands were ruined because she couldn't wash off the dirt and stain.

During winter days, the men made and repaired wagons, harnesses, and furniture. Tom and Zack each worked with loving hands on cradles and joshed each other about whose was the better one.

In the house on cold, snowy afternoons and evenings, Allena, Mary Lou, and Hattie sat around the big kitchen fireplace rubbing animal hides into softness so that they could be cut, fit, and sewn or laced into leather jackets, leggings, hats, and fur mittens. Buffalo hides were made into rugs and sleigh robes.

One winter evening when the men had gone for a few

days to check on the cattle, Allena, Mary Lou, and Hattie sat in rocking chairs around the warm kitchen fireplace making baby clothes.

"Look." Mary Lou held up a flannel dress, bonnet, and booties she'd just finished. She had crocheted a dainty edging around the neck, sleeves, and bottom hem.

Darcy, sitting close to the fire to keep warm, reached for the dress and held it up, her eyes misty. "I wish I could make something like this for my baby."

Hattie's mouth dropped open in surprise, then quickly closed into a poker face. Allena and Mary Lou glanced at each other and smiled.

"I'll help you," Mary Lou said. She walked to a chest, took out another piece of flannel, cut it into pieces for a dress, and showed Darcy how to sew the parts together.

That baby's dress opened the door for Darcy's joining the family. Much to the women's surprise, Darcy caught on fast. She appeared one afternoon with several of her dresses and cut baby clothes out of the skirts. She made one lovely sateen dress into a christening dress embroidered with minute, exquisite stitches. The other women were vocal in their praise.

"I learned all this in finishing school in Boston," Darcy confided one evening. She laughed. "I never thought I'd use it on baby clothes! It was supposed to decorate dining linens, dress collars, pillows, and pictures. I really like to do it."

A refreshing window opened into Darcy. On the men's shirts and women's shirtwaists, she made sturdy or delicate buttonholes.

"I hate to make buttonholes." Hattie squinted her nose.

"I just use overcast stitches. Ain't so pretty, but they make a hole to get a button through and that's all that's needed."

Allena, charmed at the fresh insight into her daughter-in-law, gave Zack a long list of supplies—yard goods, yarn, needles, embroidery thread, and buttons—to bring back from Harness. During morning prayer time with Mary Lou, she expressed her thankfulness for Darcy's noticeable change of heart, and they prayed that someday Darcy might feel her need for a Savior and join them in morning prayers.

seven

A blood curdling scream cut through the quiet night.

Tom and Mary Lou bolted upright in bed. Tom bounded out and hopped around on one foot, then the other, getting into his pants. He grabbed a shirt and ran barefoot out the door and down the hall. Mary Lou slipped quickly into a wrapper, stuffed her feet into slippers, and hurried after him.

Another scream. It was Darcy.

They found Zack, eyes betraying panic, nervously pacing in front of the bedroom door. "Wish we could have found Dr. Mike."

Mary Lou opened the door and slid through. Darcy lay on the bed, her usual well-coiffured hair tangled and soaked with perspiration, her knuckles white from gripping and pulling the sides and head of the bed. Hattie and Allena labored between her jerking legs.

Mary Lou had never actually birthed a baby, but she had been on hand many times to receive the slippery newborn from the birthing woman to clean with oil and wrap snugly in a warmed blanket. Now that she carried a baby within her, she felt it was time she learned more about the process. If she got caught alone. . . .

Mary Lou carefully watched Allena and Hattie as they pressed gently on Darcy's stomach and quietly and efficiently received the tiny head covered with black hair when it released itself from its confinement. A small body followed, caught by Hattie's waiting hands.

Allena beamed. "It's a boy!" She tied and cut the cord of her first grandson and handed him to Mary Lou, who cleaned and wrapped him and then placed the tiny baby in his grandmother's eager arms.

Allena lifted her head and closed her eyes. "Father, we thank You for this new little one whom You've given us. May we love him as You love us." Tears of joy spilled freely, her lips parted in a wide knowing smile.

"Another Zack. His grandfather would be proud." She turned and laid the tiny bundle beside Darcy. "Here's your son, Darcy."

Darcy opened her eyes. Her lips trembled as she gazed at the squirming infant beside her. She stared for a long moment, slowly raised her hand to touch him, then pulled back and turned her head, tears streaming down her face.

"You're tired, Darcy. Rest now, dear."

The eyes of the two women met. The younger eyes were tinged with bewilderment, fear, and anger; the older flooded with love and thankfulness.

Darcy buried her face in the pillow. "Take it away," she breathed in sobs. "That baby ruined me."

Allena's face filled with anguish. She lifted her tiny grandson and cradled him in her protective arms.

Mary Lou opened the door and Zack almost fell in.

Allena met Zack and placed his baby into his arms. "Here's your son, Zack."

Zack's worried face vanished as he awkwardly cupped the tiny bundle in his arms and gazed in awe. "My son," he said softly. "Zachary Thomas Langdon."

A crying moan came from the bed and erased the tender moment.

Zack frowned at his mother. "Is she—is Darcy all right?"

"She's fine but very tired after a full night's work." Allena smiled and took the baby. "Go see for yourself."

The door closed behind him, and they heard Darcy sobbing.

Probably nestled in Zack's arms, Mary Lou thought. *That's where I would want to be.* When she turned, Tom was staring at her, a serious look on his face.

"Are you going to have to go through all that?"

Mary Lou laughed. "I don't know of any other way to have a baby, do you? Women have told me it hurts while the baby's coming, but after it's born and in their arms, they don't remember it, too awed at the fruit of their labor."

The expression on Tom's face told her he was not convinced.

He'll have to see for himself, Mary Lou thought. Arm in arm, they slowly walked to their bedroom. Tom held her tightly. Mary Lou's heart flooded with love at his overt concern and protection. Behind the closed door of their bedroom, Tom enclosed her in his arms and held her tenderly. He kissed her hair and forehead and finally sought her mouth. It was a different kiss, not of passion, but compassion.

Tom whispered in her ear, "I don't want you hurt."

Mary Lou clung to him and whispered, "But this will be a good hurt. Mama always said good hurt brings great joy."

Tom placed his hand tenderly over Mary Lou's noticeably protruding stomach. "I'm going to be a father."

Mary Lou smiled and placed her hand over his. "And me a mother." She snuggled closer.

Tom grinned sheepishly. "It's a little scary, but I think we can handle it."

The ranch bell rang impatiently. Hattie had breakfast ready.

Over the next weeks, the household changed. Demands of a hungry baby went round the clock. Darcy stayed in bed much of the time, and although she still insisted that she didn't want a baby, Mary Lou walked in on her nursing little Zack and caught an undeniable expression of love on her face.

Zack came home earlier every day and Darcy came alive when Victor thundered to the ranch porch. Now Zack bounded into the house rather than spending time out at the barn joshing with the cowboys. Tex always took Victor to unsaddle and rub him down.

Doug was just the opposite. He stayed more and more in town. "Don't like crying babies," he said in protest one evening at the dinner table.

"That's just an excuse to avoid the ranch work and stay in town," Tom accused one night.

If real truth were spoken, Mary Lou thought, *Doug wanted to avoid talking to Zack and Tom.*

Harsh words often crossed the dinner table about the squatters on the south quarter. One night as they wrangled, Allena stood abruptly and slammed her fist on the table. "I forbid such talk! We're a disgrace to the Lord! His Word says in Romans 12:18, 'If it be possible, as much as lieth in you, live peaceably with all men.' That should mean double for brothers. I'll have no more of this until we can discuss it in love. Maybe then we'll solve problems."

She turned abruptly and left.

Her three sons watched their mother's receding back. They had never seen her so angry—nor so composed. They glanced sheepishly at each other.

Doug clattered to his feet. "I'm going to town. Mother is right. We'll never settle anything by shouting at each other."

Zack pinned Doug with a sharp gaze. "Or running away to town."

Doug glared at his older brother. "Everyone thinks I am a bounder and a thief. No one ever sees my side. I have always been the bad kid nobody liked."

Doug clenched his fists. "What reason have I to stay here? I have friends in town. They appreciate me."

"No one has accused you of anything," Zack snapped back. "You'd better look to your own conscience."

Doug's eyes narrowed to slits. His mouth parted, and he gritted his teeth and clenched his fist.

Tom jumped to his feet. "I think we'd better settle this in the barn. I'm sure Mother can hear us and it upsets her. I'd rather upset the horses."

Doug spun on his heel. "I'm going to town." He gave them his back and slammed the door so hard the windows rattled.

Mary Lou sat watching and aching. A breach in a family was so hard to watch. Hattie peeked in warily with the coffeepot in her hand. Zack smiled and held out his cup. "Thanks, Hattie, I need a refill."

Tom nodded and lifted his cup.

Zack sipped and shook his head. "Doug's getting doubly touchy. We must be hitting close. I'm checking out a land deal now and...." He pursed his lips and met Tom's gaze. "It doesn't look good. We might have less land than we think. Our southwest poachers are nothing compared with the whole eastern border of the ranch."

Tom sat up so quickly he almost spilled his coffee. "You found something?"

"I hope not, but it looks suspicious. A fancy dresser was checking out our eastern border. I don't know which side of the line he bought, Spenser's or ours. I'll find out tomorrow for sure."

The two brothers sipped thoughtfully, worry lines denting their foreheads.

Darcy slid her chair back, stood, and glared at Zack. "I know I'm not supposed to have anything to say about ranch business, but if you don't get rid of him soon, none of us is going to be left with anything."

Zack's eyes narrowed, his teeth clenched. He took a deep breath and exhaled slowly. "I think we can handle it," he said calmly. He rose and moved to the back of her chair. "Are you ready to take a ride? I told Tex to hitch the buggy so we could go after supper."

Allena entered with baby Zack in her arms and gave him to Darcy. "I think your son is hungry. He can't seem to settle."

Darcy gritted her teeth. She took him from Allena's arms. "There goes my lovely ride. All this boy ever thinks of is his stomach." She swung to Zack. "You might as well know he is the only one we'll ever have. I'm never going through this again."

Zack sagged as if he had been hit.

Mary Lou swung toward Darcy and fought the urge to shake her until her teeth rattled. Armed with an arsenal of sharp words, Darcy threw them like daggers with wanton abandon. For a while during the winter, Mary Lou had thought Darcy had softened and changed. Mama's words gentled her spirit: Only Jesus can tame a wild, selfish heart.

Oh Lord, Mary Lou prayed silently. *There's a sweet girl somewhere inside Darcy. I have had a few glimpses. Surely she couldn't have meant what she said. She's just—*

"I want to go home for a visit." With that abrupt announcement, Darcy turned on her heel and left the room to feed baby Zack.

Mary Lou followed Darcy to see if she could help.

eight

Except for feeding baby Zack, Darcy paid little attention to him. She kept reminding Allena that she wanted the baby to have a wet nurse as soon as possible. "In Boston," she said at breakfast after the men left the table, "we have nursemaids to care for babies and children so it doesn't curtail the mother's activities."

Mary Lou suppressed a smile. What activity? Other than dressing and undressing two or three times a day, eating, and going to town with Zack or on a buggy ride in the evening, Darcy kept herself to the bedroom or went on solitary walks. Darcy's congeniality and friendship with Mary Lou had cooled after baby Zack was born.

Morning devotions with Allena over, Mary Lou returned to her bedroom and opened Mama's big chest. Many of her dresses didn't fit around her waist so she decided to pack them away and wear Mrs. Cassidy's "balloon dresses," as Darcy called them. In a rare visit to Mary Lou's room, Darcy, arms full, gladly dumped the lot on Mary Lou's bed.

"I will not be wearing these anymore." Her nose wrinkled as if they were distasteful. "You can keep them."

Mary Lou was grateful. They were much more comfortable. She had bought material to sew a couple larger dresses to accommodate her growing stomach, but now she would save the cloth and make herself a new dress for church after the baby was born.

She closed the lid of the chest and glanced out the window. What a lovely April morning! She decided to take a walk to see if there were any spring flowers in bloom. Mama had always kept a bouquet of fresh prairie flowers in the vase Grandmother Stafford had sent from Toledo. Other bouquets, Mama arranged in Mason jars and set anywhere she could find a spot.

Mama's vase! Mary Lou reopened the trunk, slid her hand down inside, and felt around. She remembered Aunt Tibby rolling the vase in a blanket when they packed for Texas and snuggling it with clothes to cushion it.

Suddenly Mary Lou's hand bumped something hard. She pulled it up and removed the blanket. For the first time in a long time, tears gushed to the surface. She held the vase gently in her arms as she would have held Mama, her heart aching with the wish that Mama could be with her to see the baby born. Mama would have birthed it!

Mary Lou put the blanket back in the trunk and closed the lid. On her walk, she'd find something to put in Mama's vase.

But that wasn't the only reason she wanted to go for a walk. There was a certain place she wanted to see again.

Last night she and Tom had taken a stroll "to my favorite spot," he had said. They had stopped on a broad knoll and looked all around. The horse barns and corrals of the Circle Z were about three-quarters mile away.

"I like this place," Tom had said. "It has a good all-round view and is graded about right for a ranch house."

"A ranch house?" Mary Lou had felt exciting prickles tingle her neck. "You mean—our ranch house."

Tom had looked down at her with a silly, smug grin. "Mmm. Been thinking about it."

Mary Lou had stood on tiptoe and thrown her arms around his neck. "Oh Tom. Our own house? The main ranch house is so big, I figured we'd always live there."

"Well, there's two families plus Mother in the house now, and if Doug brings a wife and Nelson brings one, it's going to get mighty crowded." Tom had stooped down and picked her up in his arms. "Mostly I thought you might kinda like a house of your own."

Mary Lou had planted a kiss soundly on his mouth and squeezed him so hard he'd choked.

"Hold it, woman, I need to breathe."

They'd strolled back slowly in the deep twilight, full of plans. In bed, they had talked until the wee hours.

Now Mary Lou walked to the front door to go for her walk.

Darcy appeared in her morning dress.

"Going for a walk?" Mary Lou asked.

"Yes."

"Would you mind if I walked with you?"

Darcy shrugged. "If you want to."

Mary Lou stepped through the door. "It's a beautiful day. I can't stay inside."

Darcy had dressed in a delicate blue sateen with a shirred apron front that draped gracefully over her hips and met in a small bustle in the back. Mary Lou had to give her sister-in-law credit. At all costs, she fought to remain a Boston lady, even though at times it must be difficult. In her calico, Mary Lou felt like Pioneer Jane.

The two women walked east, away from the ranch.

Mary Lou decided she would wait to walk to her and Tom's special place. She breathed deeply and drank in the freshness of the spring air, almost experiencing the exhilaration of her beloved Kansas prairie wind. It was in her blood, and nothing could quite match it. Was that the way it was for Darcy? Boston must be in her blood. She must feel the same as Mary Lou felt about Venture.

"How soon will I be able to stop nursing the baby?" Darcy asked abruptly.

"It depends on the baby, mostly. And the mother. Some can be weaned around eight months, but most go about a year."

"A year! My God, I can't stand that."

Mary Lou cringed at Darcy's careless use of God's name, but she recognized desperation in her voice. God was the one Darcy needed, but the few times Mary Lou had mentioned things Mama had said about God, Darcy had stiffened and changed the subject. "Does it bother you so much to nurse him?"

"I hate it!"

Mary Lou could see it. Darcy's nose and mouth twisted in disgust.

"You're shocked?" Darcy raised her brows and smiled.

"Well. . . ." Mary Lou had to be honest. Darcy was too astute to be fooled. "Yes, but then again no. I've been brought up with it and don't think anything of it. If I had been brought up like you, maybe I'd think like you do."

Darcy stopped.

Mary Lou turned to face her. "It's just like making bread. I helped Mama make bread from the time I was a little girl, so the feel of the dough and the greasing of the pans doesn't bother me. But it did you. You don't like to touch the dough, let alone knead and shape it. Things are a little different here in Texas for me, but for you, they are a lot different." Mary Lou shrugged her shoulders. "I guess it's just what you get used to."

Darcy's penetrating gaze searched Mary Lou's innermost being. Finally, she turned back to their walk. "There's nothing here for me," she said softly. "I don't fit in like you do."

"But you have Zack. He's here for you. You love him, don't you?"

Darcy stared at Mary Lou for a moment, then sauntered over to a fallen log under a cottonwood tree and sat down. "I loved him in Boston. He was a gentleman and moved well in our society. He fit in, he knew the other men, we had the same interests. Here, he's not Zack. He's not my Zack—not the man I fell in love with." She sniffed and pulled a dainty handkerchief from the underside of her sleeve. Tears rolled down her cheeks.

Mary Lou, speechless, had never seen this Darcy, vulnerable, hurting, miserable. Darcy had everything to live for, but she didn't recognize it. What did she want? The joy of marriage was being with the one you loved. It didn't matter where, who was around, or what you were doing. If the one you loved was happy, you were happy. If they were sad, so were you. Mary Lou loved being with Tom. It didn't matter where they lived as long as they were together.

"But Zack loves you more than anything," Mary Lou protested.

"No, he doesn't." Darcy shook her head. "If he loved

me, he would have accepted the position in my father's law firm. Why did he want to be a lawyer? To potsy around in a desolate place like this when he could have become a judge someday?"

"Potsy? Is that what you think Zack is doing? Oh, Darcy. Zack is trying to bring law and order to Texas—to Harness in particular—so everyone can live in peace on their own property and not have some of the eastern land speculators rob us blind."

"Eastern land speculators! Why eastern? They come from all over."

Mary Lou had hit a nerve. "I didn't mean Boston particularly. I meant they come from everywhere east of Texas." Mary Lou thought she'd better change the subject. She didn't want to lose Darcy now. This was the best talk they'd ever had.

But Darcy was finished. She rose indignantly and marched toward the house.

Mary Lou followed her, but the weight she carried in her stomach slowed her down, and Darcy soon outdistanced her.

That afternoon, Laura rode in and invited everyone, cowboys and all, to a big barbecue. Darcy, to the surprise of the whole family, offered to stay home and take care of Baby Zack.

"Oh but I want to show off my new grandson," Allena exclaimed. "Please, Darcy, come with us."

"Take him. Zack can bring him home when it's time to eat." Darcy started for the bedroom.

Zack followed her and pleaded, "Darcy, I'd like you to go with me."

"I don't like barbecues. I don't like the meat. It's too greasy and—"

"There will be lots of other things to eat."

Darcy stretched to her tallest. "Zack, I am not going!" She swung around and walked away from him.

"But Darcy. . . ."

She spun back, her eyes flashing, fury mounting. "How am I supposed to say it so you'll understand. I'll say it again! Listen this time! I-am-not-going!" Her skirt snapped a period on her statement as she flounced around the chair and headed for their bedroom. "Take your son and bring him back when he needs Mama."

The family remained uncomfortably silent, wishing they could disappear rather than see Zack so humiliated. He stood stiff, nostrils flared, until Darcy left the room. Then his shoulders crumpled and he dipped his head. No one said anything. They stood beside him, hurting with him.

"Hattie!" Allena called.

Hattie entered immediately and glanced around the room.

"Is everything packed to go?"

"Yes'm."

Allena took a deep breath. "Then let's all get going. Mary Lou, will you please get baby Zack."

The paralyzed family snapped to attention and went their various ways to gather and assemble. Tom on Tinder and Zack on Victor took the lead. Shortly, the wagon, driven by Nelson and carrying Allena, baby Zack, Mary Lou, Hattie, and two baskets of food to contribute to the

barbecue, moved under the Circle Z arch and turned west
toward the Shepard's Bar-S ranch.

nine

Dr. Mike's faithful Betsy trotted under the Circle Z arch, headed for the hitching rail, and stopped. The doctor flopped the reins, climbed out of the buggy, and leisurely walked to the kitchen door. Hattie swung it open and greeted him with a wide, welcoming smile.

"Well, and here's my favorite girl." Dr. Mike grinned as Hattie shook her finger at him. "They say the easiest way to a man's heart is through his stomach, and your cookin' sure does touch my stomach. Someday, I'm going to ask you to marry me."

Like a flustered school girl with her first beau, Hattie ducked her head and twittered. "Oh, Dr. Mike, you're always joking."

Allena and Mary Lou entered the kitchen.

"I thought I heard your voice," Allena said. "What brings you out here? Nobody sick in this family that I know of."

Dr. Mike sat down at the kitchen table. "Now if someone was to kindly offer me a good, hot cup of coffee, I think I might have strength enough to give you an answer."

Hattie jumped up immediately and set a steaming cup of coffee before him, surrounded by a pitcher of cream and the sugar bowl. He dumped two spoons of sugar and a generous amount of cream in the cup, stirred, and sipped.

"Mmm. Now a couple good pieces of your homemade

bread with some applesauce on it might just settle my stomach."

Everyone laughed. Hattie moved and it was done. Allena and Mary Lou joined the doctor at the table.

Allena raised her cup to her lips and gazed through the steam. "You haven't answered my question. Perhaps if you give the right answer I might invite you to stay for dinner."

Dr. Mike's head bobbed a courteous bow. "I accept." He concentrated on stirring his coffee some more, and then looked straight into Allena's eyes. "I want to talk to you about baby Zack."

"Is there something wrong?" The words choked her.

"Darcy and Zack brought him to show him off when they were in town the other day. While there, Darcy changed his diaper and he began to cry. It wasn't a usual baby cry—it was a hurt cry—so I examined him. I noticed that the bottom half of his body swung to the left side, the left leg in particular. I asked Darcy if he usually cried when she changed him. She said most times."

Allena's face drained of color. "But he's just new and hasn't gotten straightened out yet."

"Allena, you know better than that. Did you notice anything unusual when you birthed him?"

Allena frowned and shook her head. "He was all curled up and seemed to straighten out when I gave his bottom a smack to catch his breath."

"You didn't notice if his body swung to one side?"

Allena's lips trembled. "As far as I could tell, it was a normal birth. He came out head first, his body followed."

"That's right." Hattie nodded.

Dr. Mike looked at Mary Lou. "Did you notice any swing to the left when you cleansed him?"

Mary Lou shook her head. "Most babies are so curled up right after they are born, it's hard to tell much of anything about what they look like stretched out."

"What's wrong, Dr. Mike?" Allena's eyed darkened. "Something is wrong, isn't there?"

He picked up the coffee pot and poured another steaming cup. "I examined him, and I believe his left leg is shorter than the right one."

Disbelief flooded Allena's pale face. Not another one! That was what old Doc Lamb had told her about Nelson. Baby Zack like Nelson?

Mary Lou slipped her arm around Allena's shoulders.

"It is just the one leg. The other seems sound as a dollar. It's not as serious as Nelson's condition. But his left leg is shorter, and that'll give him a definite limp. Of course, as he grows and uses it, he could learn to walk in a way to camouflage it."

Allena sat drained, motionless.

She'll take this in stride like everything else, Mary Lou thought. *Like Mama. Sometimes things stunned Mama, but they never defeated her. Allena is the same.* Even in her short lifetime, Mary Lou had seen many pioneer women engulfed in life-threatening danger, filled with fear and foreboding, but they had stood strong and firm.

"Then if I massage his leg like I did Nelson's, will that help?"

Dr. Mike placed his hand over Allena's limp one. "The massaging you did for Nelson is why he is able to get around as well as he does. Yes, it will help a whole lot.

That's why I wanted to talk to you first. Do the same, and baby Zack might never need crutches."

Mary Lou watched her mother-in-law slump, straighten, then draw a deep breath and pull herself under control.

"Do Darcy and Zack know about this?"

"No, that's why I came today. I saw Zack in town and he told me he was coming home at noon for dinner. Says he wants to spend some time with his boy. I thought this would be the right time and place to tell them."

Allena nodded slowly.

Mary Lou ached for Allena. Her first grandchild. *O Lord, give her strength,* she prayed.

Allena raised her chin and smiled. "Then the Lord has given baby Zack a special gift that will be enhanced by any handicap."

Mary Lou's heart swelled with pride in her new mother. She sounded just like Mama. No matter what happened, Mama had always faced it squarely.

A rider pounded into the ranch yard and Zack burst through the door grinning. "Where's my boy?" He stopped short when he saw Dr. Mike and strode over to shake his hand. "I caught you Doc. Bet you're out here for some of Hattie's good cookin'!"

Dr. Mike smiled and gripped his hand. "And to talk to you."

Zack patted Doc on the shoulder. "I'll be right back. Gotta see my boy!" He crossed the kitchen with three long strides and then bounded down the hall.

Allena's gaze swept Dr. Mike, Mary Lou, and Hattie. Then she smiled. "Baby Zack is going to be all right. I'm going to see to it."

Zack entered carrying his son, Darcy at his heels. Mary Lou noticed Dr. Mike's lips purse and a frown dent his brow. Would he rather have talked to Zack alone?

Zack settled himself and his son. "Now what did you want to talk to us about?"

Dr. Mike looked from one to the other. "Darcy," he began. "Remember when you were in my office and your baby cried when you changed him? I noticed then that his left leg is not quite right."

Fear leaped into Zack's eyes and filled his face.

"You mean my son isn't perfect?" Darcy exclaimed.

"Let me tell you first what I discovered."

Zack's brows nervously moved up and down. His jaw clenched and released as Dr. Mike explained what was wrong with baby Zack. He turned to Darcy. "If you massage him like your mother did Nelson, that will help a lot. He may have a slight limp, but he will probably learn to swing in his walk so it won't be noticeable."

Darcy's eyes grew wide and wild. "You mean baby Zack is going to be crippled like Nelson?"

"That's not the worst thing in the world that could happen."

Everyone turned to the door where Nelson stood on his crutches, grinning. Allena rose immediately and walked to her son's side, her face pained for him.

"Mother's right. She told me that God gave me something that would compensate. I love to draw and paint. I really do. If I had been normal, I would have probably killed myself bucking broncos." His eyes twinkled as he smiled. "Now I paint them."

What a brave speech, Mary Lou inwardly cheered. Her

love for her sensitive brother-in-law poured from within her toward him. Nelson's gaze turned to Mary Lou and their eyes met in mutual understanding. Mary Lou nodded. The times they had spent together had made each more sensitive to the other.

"What on earth ever made him that way?" Darcy was defensive. "My family doesn't have anyone crippled." She looked at Allena.

Darcy's sharp barb fell on dead ears. "There is no sense in searching why," Allena answered. "Or who's to blame."

Mary Lou's mind kept tugging at thoughts of Darcy's ride out alone and her fall from the horse. Could that have. . .?

Dr. Mike turned to Darcy. "Your mother worked and massaged Nelson's legs which strengthened them so he could walk with the crutches. She'll show you what she did. That will help a great deal to keep the leg stimulated and strengthen the muscles."

Darcy stared at Dr. Mike as if he were a stranger. She turned abruptly and left the room without a word. Mary Lou had an urge to follow her, but did not. Darcy was in no reasoning mood.

Zack rose, handed baby Zack to his mother, and followed her.

Dr. Mike pushed back his chair. "Zack told me one of your cowboys took a bad fall from a horse. I think I'll go check on him."

The three women watched him go out the door, grab his bag from the buggy, and head for the bunkhouse.

No one said a word. Hattie picked up the cups and took them to the washing table.

"Hattie, let the dishes be." Allena, holding baby Zack close to her heart, slid off the chair to her knees.

Mary Lou and Hattie knelt beside her.

"Dear Lord in heaven, baby Zack is Your gift to us. We know that Your love for him is far greater than ours. Now You have given us the task of caring for him to make his body stronger and to discover why You honored us by sending him to us."

Mary Lou's heart stood at attention. Honored by a baby being crippled? Remembrance triggered the voice of Big Jon's prayer the day his son, Georgie, had been needlessly shot in a shootout in front of the saloon in Venture. Mary Lou had been amazed at the lack of anger in his voice. The words that giant of a man prayed, surrounded by his questioning, frightened children, would forever echo in her ears: "I don't know how God will use this for good, but as Christians, we believe that God loves us. Even when we don't understand, we have faith that God will make it right."

Allena and Mama had that same kind of holding faith—no matter what happened.

In Venture, good had come from the spark of Georgie's death. It motivated the women to ignite and smash the saloon so that their men would have to build it outside the town line.

Little Georgie was a hero of Venture just as much as any soldier who gave his life in the Civil War. He had died for his home to make it a safer, better place.

ten

A bright, new day and a fresh breeze caressed Mary Lou
as she stepped outside the kitchen door. Breakfast over,
her bread set to rise, she moved toward the barn to find
Tom. He had mentioned the cradle was almost finished.

She felt like a clumsy, waddling goose and locked her
hands under her stomach to help carry its weight. Her time
must be close. For the last three days, her back had ached
constantly.

The familiar smells of the barn sent her thoughts back
to Kansas. Jenny's letter yesterday had bubbled with
happiness about her new married life with Glenn and how
Venture had changed since the saloon no longer dominated Main Street. Twinges of homesickness surfaced.
Jenny had written about how Glenn had changed the store
and how she loved being postmistress. Fondly Mary Lou
pictured those familiar places where she and Mama had
spent so much time together. Those had been good days,
but now. . . .

"I really would like to ride, Tom."

Mary Lou stopped. Darcy's voice? She stretched her
neck, peered over the stalls, and gasped. Darcy and Tom
were at the other end and—and Darcy had her arms around
Tom's neck! His back was to her and it looked like he—

"I love you, Tom." The words echoed back from the day
Tom had carried Darcy from his horse to her bedroom, the

day she had ridden out alone and fallen from the horse, and he'd found her. "I prayed you would come. . . ."

"Sorry, I can't leave right now, Darcy. Maybe later."

Mary Lou pressed herself against the stall. Maybe later? She couldn't breathe, her knees trembled and threatened to fold. *I've got to get out of here.* Wild eyes scanned the distance between where she stood and the door. Her body felt like a heavy, immovable stone. *I'll never make it.*

"Then get Tex or somebody else to go with me. In Boston, I rode every morning. Please, Tom," she coaxed, "please, I—"

Her words stopped! What was happening? Mary Lou felt like tearing back to rip Darcy's arms from around Tom's neck. She slowly pulled herself up and gazed over the stall.

Tom's hands were loosening Darcy's from around his neck. "Tex is out on the range this morning. The only one left here is Jess. You'll just have to wait until Zack comes home."

Mary Lou closed her eyes, eased out of sight, and blew out a silent sigh of relief. Tom's voice held a tolerance— and a finality.

Shame flooded her. *Oh, Tom, forgive me.* She should know Darcy by now. That girl would do anything to get her own way. Instead Mary Lou had mistrusted Tom!

The stomp of Darcy's boots echoed her displeasure. "In Boston, men are gentlemen," she tossed back.

Mary Lou waited a moment to compose herself before she continued on her way to Tom. When he saw her, his face lit with delight. He immediately dropped his tools and encircled her in his arms. Mary Lou dissolved in tears and clung.

Tom gently pushed her back and gazed into her face. "You all right?"

Sobbing, she nodded and tried to push a trembly smile into place.

Tom guided her to an old stool and dropped to his knees in front of her. "Darling, what's wrong?"

"Nothing's wrong. It's just me." Mary Lou threw her arms around his neck. "Forgive me, Tom."

"Forgive you? For what?"

Between sniffs and broken sentences she related to Tom what she'd seen and what she'd thought.

Tom stood, exploded into laughter, and pulled Mary Lou up into his arms. "I hope I have shown better taste in women than Darcy. Don't cry over Darcy."

"I'm not crying over her. It's me. I mistrusted you!"

Tom held her close as he could, but her stomach kept them apart. After shifting a few times, they both began laughing.

"I'm just as eager for that baby to come as you are, but for different reasons."

Mary Lou blushed. The couple wrapped arms around each other and started out of the barn.

"How about us riding out to see our place? I've got a few more ideas. Want to help me plan?"

"Oh, yes." Mary Lou watched Tom hitch Buttons to one of the buggies.

"This should be a little more comfortable. You'll have some shade. That sun is deceiving."

The road was rutted and bumpy. In truth, it couldn't boast of being a road at all. Wobbly grooves had been creased into soft wet clay from hundreds of wagon wheels and the sun had turned them into solid rock.

Tom let Buttons take her head and pick her way.

Land stretched everywhere, dotted by thousands of longhorn cows that formed moving patches of brown and white as they grazed. Texas had grown on Mary Lou. She was beginning to see the beauty Tom talked about. He stood tall when he talked of the Circle Z, thankful to his father who had poured his life's blood into making the ranch one of the largest, most productive spreads in north-central Texas.

"Are we going to build our own barns?" Mary Lou asked as they stood on their knoll and gazed across the landscape.

"Oh, yes." Tom answered. "I intend to raise horses as well as cattle. My father's reputation for fine stallions is known even in the East. He raised the best horses in these parts, and I want to do the same."

Allena's voice echoed in Mary Lou's mind: *Tom has his father's heart.* Mary Lou swelled with pride, joy and— "Ohhhh!" She doubled over in pain and sank to the ground.

Tom caught her in his arms and carried her to the buggy. "I think we'd better head back."

The road appeared rougher than when they came. Every bump hammered Mary Lou's back, while periodic pains stabbed her stomach. The trip lasted an eternity.

When the buggy reached the ranch, Tom bounded out and hollered for Hattie. She appeared at the door, took one look at Tom carrying Mary Lou, and disappeared.

Within seconds, Allena came.

By the time Tom carried Mary Lou into the bedroom, Hattie had the bed open and ready. She scurried out to fill her tub and boil water.

Tom helped his mother undress Mary Lou and get her into a large gown. When he was satisfied that his wife was settled, Tom pulled up the chair and sat beside her.

Pains began coming harder and more often. Mary Lou gritted her teeth and moaned. She smiled at Tom, thinking to ease the pain she saw in his anxious face.

Allena put her hand on Tom's shoulder. "Son, it would be better if you left. We women can take care of everything."

Mary Lou felt Tom's hands on her face and his kiss on her forehead. She smiled weakly. "Pretty soon, Tom, our—" Her words were cut off by a sharp pain that rhythmically brought on another and another.

"Now git." Allena took her son by the arm and led him to the door. "Things are happening fast. I don't think it will be too long. I'm surprised she was able to bump over the road." She laughed. "That's probably what started everything."

Never had Mary Lou endured such pain. Her body writhed in protest. Hattie kept wiping her face with a cool cloth.

After what seemed like hours, Allena hollered, "Now, push, Mary Lou. Push!"

Her body ripped in half.

"It's a boy!" Mary Lou heard Allena call out, then laughter filled the room.

A boy. Her swimming head cleared at the joyous news. She laughed with them. A son for Tom. Mary Lou took a deep breath. It was over.

Suddenly the hammer of pain pounded her body again.

She heard Allena and Hattie talking, but the hurt mumbled their words. Mary Lou gasp as another pain tore at her, then another and another.

"Mary Lou!" Allena's voice came from a deep well.

She dragged open bleary eyes. Her mother-in-law's face was close to hers.

"Bear down again, Mary Lou. Hard. Do you hear me? Bear down again."

Again? But she was done. A fresh pain stabbed her lower parts. Would it ever be over? It didn't seem Darcy had had such a time, or was it just that Mary Lou was the one hurting this time?

"Mary Lou, stop screaming and push!"

Allena's words shattered in her head and her body convulsed, but Mary Lou pushed—and pushed. She heard a baby cry and Allena and Hattie laughing. It boggled her mind. Finally her body settled into peace and everything went black.

eleven

Mary Lou forced open heavy eyelids. Blurred figures surrounding the bed evolved into shapes.

Tom stood with a baby in each arm. He leaned over, kissed her, laid a baby on each side of her, and raised up grinning. "How about this, little Mama? We have twins, a boy and a girl."

In awe, Mary Lou gazed from one small bundle to the other, then into the proud, adoring eyes of her husband. "Oh, darling," she cried. "The Lord gave us hundredfold!" She laughed until it hurt, her gaze devouring one small pink face, then the other.

Little Tom's head was hazed with red and looked just like his father. Beth's hair was longer and the color of Mama's. Twins! Even seeing them, Mary Lou couldn't believe it!

Allena opened each blanket to expose tiny legs and arms. She patted Beth. "She took us by surprise. Little Tom came, and then you went into labor again and out came this tiny little girl who screamed as if she thought we'd forgotten her." Allena leaned over and kissed Mary Lou on the forehead. "Thank you, my dear. That puts three arrows in my quiver."

Tom helped Mary Lou sit up, lifted the babies into her arms, and sat beside her with his arms around his family.

Mary Lou touched and rubbed their soft, tiny legs and

hands. "I wish Mama were here to see them." She felt Tom's arm tighten around her.

Allena smiled. "And who's to say she doesn't know? I'm sure in heaven she's as pleased and happy as I am with our two beautiful grandchildren."

"Thank you, Mother."

Hattie came in with a bowl of steaming soup. "If you're going to nurse two, you'd better start eating." She handed the bowl to Tom.

Allena took the twins, while Hattie added plump pillows to help Mary Lou sit up straight to eat.

A knock sounded on the door, and Darcy peeked in. "I came to see what all the fuss is about."

Mary Lou's heart warmed. "Come in, Darcy, and look what the Lord sent!"

Darcy's lips formed a noncommittal smile.

Did Mary Lou read a longing in Darcy's dark eyes? It vanished as quickly as it came. "Won't baby Zack, little Tom, and Beth have fun playing together?"

"I'm glad for you," Darcy said with genuine compassion.

Their eyes met. For the first time, Mary Lou felt kin to Darcy. They were both mothers. She sensed a desolate ache and longed to put her arms around Darcy as she had Nelson. Darcy dropped her gaze. A second later she looked up. The veiled Darcy was back.

Three small babies kept things buzzing day and night. Hattie tried to keep up with the baby laundry, and for the first time, she couldn't seem to keep a supply of hot water.

Tom stayed close to home as much as he could and tended to needed jobs around the barn, stables, and ranch house. Mary Lou often put the twins in baskets, and they each carried one to the barn just to be together. Tom worked steadily on a cradle for Beth, who seemed quite comfy in a makeshift bed in the bottom drawer of Mama's chest.

Darcy dressed and fed baby Zack, but Allena did the therapy on his leg. She tried to teach Darcy but Darcy refused to learn.

One day the young mothers sat in the rockers on either side of the fireplace in the kitchen, their babies in their laps. Hattie loved their company and usually found a job she could do sitting in her rocking chair.

She surprised them that morning by confiding, "I had a little son when I was about your age."

Mary Lou exclaimed, "Hattie! I didn't know you were ever married." Hattie sat and nodded, seemingly lost in her task of paring potatoes. Softly she spoke. "My man, Jeremy, was killed in the Civil War. I tried to keep our farm in Pennsylvania going for Sonny and me. When he was killed—"

Mary Lou gasped. "Killed! Oh, how old was he?"

Hattie heaved a painful sigh. "Four. I was busy working in the garden and didn't notice him wander into the woods." She dropped her hands into her lap, mindless of the knife and partially peeled potato, and stared into the painful memory.

Mary Lou sensed her anguish. "What happened?"

"I heard a bear growl, then Sonny's scream. I jumped up and ran into the woods." Hattie voice broke.

"After a bear?" Mary Lou exclaimed. "Oh, Hattie, I would be scared to death." Neither she nor Darcy asked the next question.

Hattie gathered a corner of her apron to capture her tears. "All I found was his torn bloody clothes." Her voice grew soft and husky. "I buried them in a grave and left the farm."

"How did you ever get here from Pennsylvania?"

"I got on the first stage headin' west. Mr. Langdon was on the stage, and he kindly became my protector. After I told him my story, he said his wife had been hunting for a housekeeper and asked if I would consider the job. I came to see and stayed." Hattie peeled another potato. "I know as well as I sit here, it was God's providence."

Mary Lou's neck tingled.

Later, out in the barn, Mary Lou told Tom.

Tom nodded. "I remember when she came. I was about four or five. She was the one I always ran to when Doug would pick on me."

Mary Lou remembered her first conversation with Hattie. "Mr. Tom, he's special," she had said. Now Mary Lou knew why.

"There, it's finished." Tom gave Beth's cradle a final polish with a cloth. "Now I can concentrate on the cattle drive. Smitty and the boys have been getting things ready for that long trip to Abilene. We'll be leaving next week."

Mary Lou dreaded the thought of Tom being gone for a couple months. She knew it was impossible, but she longed to go home for a visit. The thought of seeing Aunt Nelda, Aunt Tibby, Jenny, Glenn, and her father filled her with her worst case of homesickness since she had left home. Yet she knew the twins were much too small to travel that long distance.

"Perhaps after the spring roundup next year," Tom suggested, "the twins will be old enough to travel and we can head to Kansas for a visit. How would that be?"

Mary Lou threw her arms around her dear husband who so often seemed to sense what she thought. At times it was a little scary, but in truth, she knew love could do that. She remembered Mama and Pa before his accident broke the connection.

Stacey's Manner 111

Carolyn tell the truth, Looking past Mary Lou, she said, "The twins will be old enough for me to care..."

...looked in question after a while they wouldn't find...

Mary Lou's...

twelve

The day before Tom, Smitty, and the boys left on the cattle drive, Mary Lou and Hattie scrubbed over washboards all day in between the needs of the twins. At the moment, Tommy and Beth were both asleep in their cradles—a rare phenomenon.

Line after line of clean clothes had fluttered in a gentle, warm morning wind and dried quickly. The two women caught and pulled the dry clothes from the line, separated the baby clothes, piled them all in two laundry baskets, and carried them toward the house.

A shiny new buggy rolled into the yard and stopped at the hitching rail. Doug got out and ran around to the passenger side.

Hattie motioned with her head. "Looks like Mr. Doug bought himself a new buggy." She continued toward the kitchen door and then stopped. Mouth open, eyes wide, Hattie stared.

The same expression covered Mary Lou's face.

Brazenly hanging on Doug's arm was a girl from the saloon! Mary Lou couldn't believe it. One of those women? Why would Doug bring her here? His mother would be shocked!

Hattie's mouth closed into a pursed line of fury. Her eyes spit fire. Mary Lou hurriedly opened the kitchen door, and Hattie stomped through, plunking the basket on the

112

floor. "I knew that boy had a lot of nerve, but this is too much. Shows no respect for his mother at all."

Allena entered the kitchen as the front door banged.

"We have company" was all Mary Lou could think to say.

"Good." Allena moved toward the parlor to greet them. Mary Lou followed gingerly.

Doug strutted in, the girl slightly behind him and noticeably uneasy. He stood, a sly grin on his face, and looked at Allena. "Mother, this is my wife, Lily." He pulled the girl from behind him and thrust her forward. "Sorry we didn't have time for her to change from her wedding gown."

Allena raised to her full height and nodded slowly.

The new bride wore a short, flouncy ruffled dress and high-heeled, lacy shoes. A black Spanish fringed shawl covered her bare shoulders, the ends clutched tightly in her hands.

Thunderbolts exploded in Mary Lou's head. Doug married to her?

Allena hesitated only a second. Irrespective of what must have been going through her mind, she graciously stepped forward and stretched both hands toward her new daughter-in-law.

"I thought since Zack and Tom surprised you with a bride, I could do no less." Doug laughed.

Allena reprimanded her son with a sharp glance, accepted Lily's hesitant hands, smiled, and placed a gentle kiss on her cheek. She turned to Doug. "When were you married?"

"This morning. We thought we better make it legal so

we went to a justice of the peace."

Mary Lou watched a disturbing shadow cross Allena's face and her heart ached for her. For a Christian, marriage without clergy was no marriage at all.

Allena linked her arm through Lily's. "Come, my dear."

At Allena's touch, Lily drew herself to full height.

Mary Lou marveled at the composure and dignity her mother-in-law displayed. Three of her sons had ignored any plans she may have had for them and married absolute strangers.

"I'm sure you would feel more comfortable if you changed out of your wedding dress." Allena turned to Mary Lou. "Lily looks about your size and should fit one of your dresses, don't you think?" Allena guided Lily toward the bedrooms.

Doug folded his arms, his mouth a twisted grin of malicious pleasure.

Mary Lou shuddered. He was enjoying the situation— had created it deliberately! For what reason? To hurt his mother? What cruel quirk chewed at him inside and fanned an inner war that made him enjoy hurting others? At home he constantly put everyone on edge and changed the whole atmosphere of the household.

Hattie must have been glued to the dining room door frame. She appeared the minute Allena and Lily left and gazed down the hall at their retreating figures. "Well, I never—"

Doug walked over and put his arm around Hattie's shoulders. "What's the matter, Hattie, don't you approve of my new wife?"

Incensed, Hattie brushed his arm off her shoulders.

Doug's wry smile pulled his nose into a sneer. "You don't like me, do you, Hattie?"

"I'm a Christian. I love you, but I don't like the way you act. Shame on you, puttin' your ma in such a position. One of these days, Mr. Doug, you're goin' to get your come-uppance, and it won't be good."

Doug's face clouded into a scowl. "Dear Hattie. I always knew I was your favorite." He laughed.

"Humph!" Hattie grabbed the laundry basket, stomped outside, and banged the door against his laughter.

Mary Lou tiptoed quietly into her bedroom and slowly opened Mama's chest, hoping not to disturb the twins. They looked like soft, pink cherubs. She pushed aside her favorite blue dress that Mama had made and picked up a couple of her better calicos and a petticoat. She followed Hattie, who was carrying a pitcher of hot water to Doug's room. After placing the clothes on Doug's bed, Mary Lou and Allena stepped out into the hall.

They heard rustlings and splashing within. Shortly the door opened, and Lily stepped out in a long-skirted calico. Her face had been scrubbed till it shone, and her light brown, wavy hair was twisted into a high bun on top of her head.

Mary Lou stood in awe at the transformation. Lily was pretty!

Allena smiled and nodded. "That looks more comfortable." She swept her hand around Doug's room in its usual state of upheaval. "Forgive this room. Hattie and I will clean it and help you get settled."

As they entered the kitchen, Doug struggled to carry two carpet bags through the door. His eyebrows raised at Lily, and he wrinkled his nose. "Now you look like all the women. I like you better the other way." He dropped the bags in the middle of the kitchen floor.

Lily smiled, lips trembling. A horse clattered to the post.

Tom! Mary Lou thought with relief. She watched him dismount, bang the dust off himself, and stride toward the door.

Doug greeted him with a punch on the shoulder and moved him in front of Lily. "Little brother, meet my new wife." Doug moved beside Lily, put his arm around her waist, and grinned.

Tom's eyebrow arched in surprise. "You? Married? I don't believe it!" He grinned, reached out, and returned Doug's punch. "About time you settled down."

"Who said anything about settling down?"

Tom's expression exhibited the shock they all felt. Lily's lips opened for a sharp intake of breath. Her shoulders sank for a scant second, but then her chin and shoulders squared and she smiled sweetly. "You must be Tom."

Tom nodded his head and walked toward her. He picked up Lily's hand, lightly kissed it, looked up, and smiled. "Welcome, Lily."

Lily bowed her head slightly, visibly shaken. When Tom released her fingers, she withdrew her hand and held it as if she'd been given a gift.

Darcy entered, carrying baby Zack, and was introduced to her new sister-in-law. She assessed the young woman from head to foot, and then nodded in dismissal.

Lily brightened. "Oh." Her laugh jangled. "You have a baby! I love babies."

Doug eyes widened, his brows lifted, and he rolled his eyes.

Darcy held the baby forward. "You can hold him if you like."

Lily hesitated a moment, darted a glance at Doug who shrugged his shoulders, then eagerly gathered the baby into her arms.

"We have two," Mary Lou said proudly. "Tom and I have twins, a boy and a girl. They are both asleep, which doesn't happen too often or last too long. If one wakes. . . ."

Lily looked wistfully into Mary Lou's eyes. "How fortunate you are."

Doug snickered and made an exaggerated bow. "Now if you ladies can spare me, I've got to get back to town and meet a man coming in on the stage." He glanced at Darcy. "A friend of yours."

Darcy came to life. "Kenneth?"

Doug nodded. "He'll be here today hopefully with two other eastern gentlemen."

"Do bring them out!" Darcy beamed. "It will be wonderful to see Kenneth again."

Doug nodded, grabbed his hat, and aimed for the door. "Bye, Lily. See you later," he called over his shoulder. The clip-clop of his horse's hooves faded quickly.

Lily raised her hand in a short wave and turned her undivided attention to baby Zack.

"I'll be out in the barn," Tom said and left.

For a strained moment, the four women regarded one another.

Hattie moved first, toward the kitchen. "I'd best be

gettin' busy. I'm way behind in my work."

Allena pointed down the hall. "Let's see what we can do to make Doug's room presentable."

"I'll set the table, Hattie," Mary Lou called, carrying an armful of dinner plates into the dining room. She hovered over the table with the extra place setting, wondering where to put it. Allena sat at the end of the table and father Zachary's place was completely set, his chair in place at the opposite end. Zack, Darcy, Tom, and Mary Lou sat on Allena's right. Immediately to her left, Nelson had the end chair to facilitate him maneuvering his crutches. Doug came next.

Mary Lou set Lily's plate in the place next to Doug. That left one guest chair next to Lily, across from Mary Lou. She stared at it a long moment. *I wonder who will fill it?*

thirteen

Tom pulled the wagon up to the hitching rail to let Mary Lou off with the twins. They had spent the morning in their future home. Each room that took shape fulfilled something deep inside Mary Lou. Tom said as soon as the floors were in, they could prepare to move. Excitement bubbled in her heart, and she thanked God for her many blessings.

A horse thundered through the Circle Z arch. Laura, her hair stretched behind her riding the wind, came to an abrupt halt and slid to the ground, breathless, in front of Tom and Mary Lou.

"You're just the ones I want to see. I need help." Laura grabbed Tommy from Tom, and she and Mary Lou walked to the house.

Tom swung the wagon toward the barn. "I'll be back," he called over his shoulder.

Allena and Lily, carrying baby Zack, had gone to town to buy yard goods for new clothes for Lily plus a list of supplies needed by Hattie. Darcy accompanied them for a visit to the dressmaker. Kenneth Dillard fused new life into Darcy, and she spent hours eagerly making plans to return to Boston to visit her parents. Nelson clumped down the hall to greet them.

Laura ran to meet him and brazenly embraced and kissed him in front of Tom and Mary Lou. She turned smiling. "This is what I—we—want to talk to you about."

The twins had to be fed and settled for their naps before

any serious conversation could take place, but soon the four adults were gathered around the table with some dinner.

Nelson blurted out the news. "Laura and I want to get married."

Neither Mary Lou nor Tom was surprised at the announcement, but they understood the younger couple's dilemma. Allena had closed her ears to their plea.

"What does Mother say?" Tom asked.

Nelson shook his head. "She says we're both too young to handle a ranch because of my legs."

Laura tossed her head like an impatient pony. "Owning a ranch isn't the only thing in the world. We could move to Harness, have a business, or something else. I'm a good cook; we could open a boarding house."

Nelson sipped his coffee. "I always knew I would never be a rancher. Mother says God has something else for me, yet she keeps talking about me working a ranch. Other people earn a living without a ranch. I'm confident Laura and I can make it somehow."

He reached into his pocket and brought out a necklace made of dainty polished stones. "If I can sell my paintings to Mr. Dillard, I can sell these too."

Mary Lou turned the necklace over and over in her hands and draped it around her neck. "Nelson, this is lovely. When did you make this?"

"This spring. I saw a stone necklace hanging around the neck of an Indian girl in Harness. I gathered these stones around your place, polished them, scraped a hole through, and strung them."

Mary Lou's heart ached for these two young people

reaching for any straw that would enable them to have a life together. She remembered the year she yearned for Tom, not knowing whether she would ever see him again, let alone marry him. But God had answered her prayers.

She remembered her own quandary and how she had clung to Pa's arm as he led her into Aunt Tibby's parlor to be married. Her heart had wept over her lost dream, but she had resolutely resigned herself to marrying Glenn and being a town girl. Yet within that next hour, God had fulfilled her dream of being a rancher's wife. If all the bizarre obstacles she and Tom had faced were swept away to make it possible for them to marry, then there was a way God had in mind to work out a marriage for Laura and Nelson.

"How do your folks feel about it?" Tom asked Laura.

"Father and Mother have given their blessing, but they know how Allena feels. Ma says she is too protective of Nelson, that he is a grown young man now, not her little boy." Laura's eyes glistened with tears, and she shook her head vigorously and wailed, "He can't be her little boy all his life!" Tears spilled and Laura placed her hand over her mouth. "I'm sorry—that was disrespectful."

Tom gazed at Nelson. "And how do you feel about it all?"

Nelson looked up with stars in his eyes. "I love Laura, and I'm going to marry her. We'll make it. God will show us a way. I know it." He set his face.

Silence prevailed, minds churned.

Tom's voice broke through. "Are you two prepared to live here at the ranch for a while after you are married to satisfy Mother that you are capable of handling whatever comes?"

No answer was needed in light of the beaming smiles on two young faces.

"Then let's pray and look for what God has in mind. In the meantime," Tom grinned, "you two get ready to be married."

Hattie came through the kitchen door with a bag over her shoulder, a vegetable bounty from the garden. She glanced at four shining faces, grinned, plopped her bag on a chair, and faced them with that knowing look.

Tom laughed. "And what do you think about it, Hattie?"

She stifled a smile. "About what?"

"Don't pretend to me, Hattie. Your ears are wiggling."

"Oh, Mr. Tom."

Tom jumped up and put his arm around her shoulders. "Hattie, I want to know what you think about Nelson and Laura getting married."

"It's high time." She gazed at Nelson. "That young man needs a wife." She turned to Laura. "And he's not goin' to find a better one than you, Miss Laura."

Laura rose, rushed to Hattie, threw her arms around her, and planted a kiss on her cheek. "Tell that to Mother Langdon."

Hattie got all ruffled. "Now you children know me. I don't interfere."

Tom let loose a hearty laugh. "You and Mother interfere with everything that goes on around here and seemingly never make a decision."

"I've said my say." Hattie grabbed the washing pan, poured water into it, and began scrubbing vegetables vigorously.

"So you have." Tom touched her bouncing cheek and made her blush. "And we are all in agreement." He stood in thought and then bowed his head. "Now it's praying time."

Everyone bowed.

"Father God," Tom began, "You know all about us, our deepest hopes and desires. And You know all about love. You displayed it for us on the cross. We ask, Father, that our personal desires not hinder You in this matter. Thy will be done. In Jesus' name, Amen."

Head still bowed, Laura added quietly, "And help us recognize Your answer when it comes, dear Lord." She sighed. "And, please—make it soon!" She lifted damp lashes and gazed at Nelson.

Nelson cradled her gaze in his. "Amen."

A howl from one twin cut through the air, accompanied quickly by the other. Mary Lou and Laura both rose and left the kitchen. Tom and Nelson walked to the barn.

In the late afternoon, Allena and Lily drove into the yard. Mary Lou and Laura ducked through lines fluttering with baby clothes and diapers and carried the twins to meet their grandmother.

"Where's Darcy?" Mary Lou asked.

"She wanted to stay in town and come home with Zack and Mr. Dillard. Zack will rent a buggy to bring them home."

Both women climbed out of Allena's buggy and grabbed a twin. Laura and Mary Lou gathered their string-tied packages, and they all walked to the house.

Allena opened the kitchen door. "Get ready, Hattie. Mr. Dillard will be here for supper."

The evening bubbled with plans. Mr. Dillard already had arrangements for he and Darcy to leave on a stage riding north the next Monday. He couldn't leave earlier— had business to finish up, he said.

The week passed quickly. Darcy went into town twice to be fitted and to check on her new dresses and hats.

Lily took care of baby Zack and loved every minute of it. She showered him with love, and he preferred Lily to anyone else. Allena showed her how to care for the baby's leg and Lily was faithful in her treatments.

One morning, Allena and Mary Lou were in the parlor reading the Bible for morning devotions. A sudden noise caught their attention and the flip of a rustling skirt caught their eye. Mary Lou rose and went to see who it was. As she reached the door, she saw Lily's back disappearing into the kitchen.

"It was Lily passing by," she said.

Next morning, the rustling was there again. Mary Lou rose, very quietly this time, and tiptoed to the door. When she peeked around the door frame, Lily was standing with her back to the wall, listening. Mary Lou motioned Allena to come.

Allena stepped into the hall.

Startled, Lily pressed back against the wall as if she'd been caught in a crime.

Allena smiled. "Lily, would you like to come join us in our devotions?"

Lily's smile erased uneasiness. "Yes ma'am. I would."

"Then come in, my dear. You're welcome."

The three women settled themselves.

"We were just finishing the last few verses of Proverbs

31."

Lily nodded and folded her hands in her lap.

Allena picked up her Bible, smoothed the page, and continued: "She looketh well to the ways of her household, and eateth not the bread of idleness. Her children arise up, and call her blessed; her husband also, and he praiseth her. Many daughters have done virtuously, but thou excellest them all."

Mary Lou spied two fat streams of tears cascading down Lily's cheeks. Her shoulders shuddered and sobs began.

Allena looked up from her reading.

Lily covered her face with her hands. "I. . .shouldn't be. . .here. I'm. . .a. . .sinful woman. I knew—when Doug married me—I. . .shouldn't have. . . ." Sobs consumed her. She covered her head with her arms and slumped into a heap of misery.

Allena laid her Bible aside, looked tenderly at Mary Lou, and nodded. Mary Lou knelt beside Lily, put her arms around her, and cradled her head. "Don't cry, Lily, you're fine now. God has given you a whole new life."

Allena's hand smoothed Lily's hair. "This is exactly where you should be, my dear. Remember the question Jesus asked the woman caught in adultery: 'Where are your accusers?'"

Lily raised her wet, agonized face.

Allena cupped it in her hands. "No one has come forth to accuse you. Neither do we, Lily. God has given us a glimpse of your true heart."

Lily's tear-stained eyes lifted in amazement and searched first Allena's face, then Mary Lou's. Lily slipped from her chair to her knees. "Oh, God, forgive me," she cried and collapsed into tears.

Allena and Mary Lou slipped to their knees beside her.

"Father," Allena began, "Your child has come home, and she accepts Your forgiveness. There is no one here to cast the first stone."

The three women knelt in silence for a few moments then rose and hugged one another. Tears flowed freely, and each found the corner of her apron to wipe her face.

A familiar sound penetrated. Babies were crying. The women smiled, rose from their knees, and went back to work.

fourteen

The sun yawned, stretched, opened its eyes, and peeked into the new day. Golden fingers traveled across the land and encircled a young man and woman standing in front of an adobe shell of a house, snuggled into the ground by its new roof.

Tom slipped an arm around Mary Lou, grinned, and squeezed her waist. "I really wanted to be done and have us moved in before I left, but I couldn't make it. Tex and Bart are in charge while I'm gone, and they'll finish putting down the wooden floor. By the time I get back, they should be done and we can move in. The wells and root cellar were finished yesterday."

Tom gently folded his wife in his arms and gazed into her upturned face. "It used to be I could hardly wait until the trail drive began. Now I wish it was over. It's not going to be easy being away from you and the twins. I'll probably have Smitty on my back for trying to move the cows too fast, but I intend to make this the fastest trip on record." He bent and rested his lips on hers and they melted together into a soothing, gentle kiss.

Mary Lou clung to her husband to stem the surge of loneliness that came from the mere thought of him not being near. The hollow, uncomfortable feeling she remembered when he had left her at Point Lane the day Mama died returned and stabbed her heart. She had filled

127

one of Tom's pouches with letters to Aunt Tibby, Aunt Nelda, Jenny, and her father, and she had secretly included six letters for Tom with instructions for him to read one a week. She smiled. Knowing Tom, he would read them all at once and reread them many times. She would have done the same.

Tom pulled her inside the house. "I have to show you something."

Mary Lou saw it immediately, sitting in the middle of the kitchen floor. Their big, new, four-poster bed! Tom had worked on it every evening, but she hadn't realized it was done! She walked around it and ran her hands up and down the smooth posters. "It's beautiful!"

"And long enough for me to sleep with my feet in the bed."

They both laughed.

Mary Lou's gaze wandered around the two rooms. As soon as the floors were done, she would have Tex and Bart move the bed into the bedroom. Hopefully, with Allena and Lily's help, she could get the rugs for each side of the bed finished and the new patchwork quilt all backed and tied before Tom returned. Then after his long, tiring ride home, they could snuggle in their own bed in their new home.

Mary Lou's memory jumped back to the day Pa, she, and Mama had moved into their new cabin in Venture. "Always set up and make your beds first thing when you move into your new home," Mama had said. "Then they are ready for everyone to fall into after the hard day's work of settling." Mary Lou planned to do just that.

Tinder and Dulcie stood like two sentinels, patiently

awaiting their masters. Once mounted, the horses trotted eagerly back to the ranch house.

As they approached, they spied Kenneth Dillard's rented buggy at the hitching rail. They dismounted and stopped to catch voices in vigorous discussion drifting out the parlor window.

"I know your mother and father are looking forward to seeing their only grandson," Tom and Mary Lou heard Kenneth say.

"He's too young to travel all that distance," came Allena's quick reply.

"Darcy, travel is hard enough for an adult, let alone a seven-month-old baby." Zack's voice.

To announce their coming, Tom and Mary Lou opened and closed the kitchen door with a bang.

Darcy glanced up as they entered. Baby Zack was tightly cradled in his mother's arms. "I wondered if you were coming back before we left so we could say good-bye." Darcy eyed Mary Lou. "Maybe you two can help us decide this matter. Mother and Zack won't let me take my baby home to see his grandparents."

Mary Lou couldn't believe what she heard. Darcy had told her just the day before that she had no intention of taking baby Zack. Her mouth opened in surprise. "But I thought you said—"

"I know, I know," Darcy interrupted, "but Mother Langdon and Zack insist the trip will be too much for him." Darcy's dark eyes flashed Mary Lou a warning.

"The trip will be rather tough on the little fellow," Tom offered. "It's a long, bumpy, dusty ride between stations."

Mary Lou stared in disbelief at Darcy's mother act.

Darcy hugged her baby tightly to her breast as if she never wanted to let him go. She wended slowly back and forth between Zack, Allena, and Kenneth, who leaned against the wall watching her with the hint of a wry smile on his face.

Mary Lou's confusion cleared. Darcy didn't want to take baby Zack home with her. She had cunningly directed everything so it would look like she did. Mary Lou could almost guess what would happen. Soon Darcy would make a dramatic sacrifice. She would let her mother-in-law and husband have their own way, and she would win the battle with no one the wiser.

Darcy's dark, sad eyes gazed from one to the other. She raised baby Zack to her shoulder, kissed and patted him, and exuded a long, trembling sigh. After a long moment, she raised moist lashes to Zack, sandwiched their son between them, and looked repentantly into her husband's face.

"Darling, I'm sorry. I'm afraid I'm being selfish." She pressed the baby into his father's arms, lowered her head, and said softly; "Zack, you are right. The trip will be too hard on him now." She paused and looked painfully into Zack's face. "I'll wait till next time."

Mary Lou, astounded at Darcy's farce, stood grounded on the spot, her tongue glued to the roof of her mouth.

Big teardrops slipped from Darcy's eyes. She daintily reached for the lace handkerchief tucked inside her sleeve, daubed her eyes, and then stood on tiptoe and kissed Zack's cheek. "For baby Zack's sake, I'll leave him with you. I'll tell Mother and Father they will have to wait until he is old enough to travel." She turned and walked out of the room.

Both Allena and Zack eased a visible sigh. Zack held his son close and followed Darcy. Mary Lou stifled a smile. Darcy had won, but in truth she had lost. The real winner was baby Zack—and Lily.

Kenneth informed Zack the stagecoach would arrive in Harness around six o'clock in the morning. Rather than ride out so early from the Circle Z, Kenneth suggested that they arrange for a room at the hotel in Harness for Zack and Darcy to stay overnight so that Darcy could be rested before the long trip. Before supper, they piled Darcy's trunk and several carpet bags on the back of the buckboard.

A radiant Darcy presided at the supper table. Mary Lou couldn't keep her eyes off her. Nor could anyone else. This was a Darcy the family had never seen: gracious, charming, smiling, chattering, beautiful in behavior as well as in appearance. Now all could see the girl Zack fell in love with. *I don't blame him,* Mary Lou thought. From the look on Allena's face, her mother-in-law agreed.

Supper over, everyone gathered around the buggy and buckboard to say good-bye. Darcy, standing beside Mary Lou, turned abruptly, and their eyes met in a penetrating stare. Mary Lou perceived a softness, a winsomeness in Darcy she had sensed many times, but had never seen set free.

Darcy gently put her arms around Mary Lou and said softly, "Thank you for being my friend. I'm afraid I gave you a hard time, but I always admired you and have often wished I could be like you, Prairie Girl. I have a friend in Boston who is a lot like you, sweet and kind to everyone." Darcy ducked her head. "Even me. She talks about God like you do, as if He is with her every minute."

Mary Lou's heart soared. Here was her chance to speak a word about God to Darcy. Without restraint, Mary Lou threw her arms around her. "He is!" Mary Lou whispered in Darcy's ear, and then pushed her back and looked into her dark, fathomless eyes. "And He will be with you always if you let Him."

Oh God, Mary Lou prayed. *Help Darcy's godly friend to bring her to the saving grace of Jesus.*

"I'm going to miss you, Darcy." Mary Lou gave her an extra squeeze. "Hurry back," she said, and meant it.

Zack helped Darcy into the buggy with Kenneth, then climbed into the buckboard. As they trotted off, Darcy spotted Lily standing with baby Zack in her arms.

Darcy waved. "Take good care of him, Lily." she called.

"I will." Lily lifted baby Zack's arm and waved it to his mother. Everyone waved until the wagons passed under the Circle Z arch.

At four o'clock the next morning, Tom climbed out of bed, gathered his clothes, leaned over for a long look at the twins in their cradles, and tiptoed to the kitchen to get dressed.

Mary Lou, already dressed, checked the twins. Their reposed pink faces spoke of angels and fluttered her heart. She dared not touch one for fear they would wake.

Tom, Smitty, and the cowboys had ridden the range for the last month rounding up the longhorns from summer pasture and heading them north. The cowboys had been on night watch for three weeks with several good cutting horses to change the mind of any feisty bull that suddenly decided he wanted to be boss and lead off a bunch of cows.

Long before sunup, Jess, the cook, had risen to make an early breakfast of beef, sourdough biscuits, gravy, potatoes, and greens for the cowboys to stock up before they left. After cleanup, Jess drove the chuck wagon out with Smitty, the trail boss, who took the lead to find grazing land up ahead. The cowboys' job was to keep the cattle together and moving.

Mary Lou and Tom had planned to say good-bye in the parlor. She sat braiding old material into a rug and put it aside when she heard Tom's step.

Other than a few night watches when Tom had been out riding the line, they had never been apart. Neither of them said much, but both dreaded this time of parting.

Their kiss was long and sweet. Tom's arms held Mary Lou extra tight, as though he wanted to hold her forever. When he released her, Mary Lou felt cast adrift.

Tom picked up her hands and planted a kiss in each palm and closed her fingers. "Keep these until I come back, and I'll redeem them."

They went outside.

"I'll tell everyone in Venture you said hello and you miss them very much," Tom said as he mounted Tinder.

Mary Lou nodded her head. She didn't dare speak. A dam of tears awaited any release. She had determined to send Tom off with smiles and waves. She stood with her arm in motion until he blended into the landscape.

A familiar cry came from the house. Tommy. A soft gurgling voice joined him. The twins were awake.

fifteen

A month dragged by. Mary Lou shook and spread the wet clothes on the line to dry, a never-ending job with three babies. Lily came around the side of the house carrying another full basket.

"We're going to have to string another line," Mary Lou hollered.

Lily dropped her basket, spun on her heel, and shortly emerged with more rope. She strung it between two poles and proceeded with her task of tossing and smoothing the wet clothes over the line.

A familiar horse and rider pounded through the arch. Doug reined abruptly, sending a dust swirl into the air that innocently settled on the clean wash.

Lily ran to meet him, all smiles. "You're home early."

He slid to the ground and dropped the reins. "Not for long," he said and strode in giant steps toward the door.

By the time Mary Lou and Lily walked into the kitchen, they heard Doug in the ranch office, slamming drawers and mumbling to himself. "Where is it?" he shouted.

The two women, surprised to see the office door standing open, watched Doug as he scattered papers everywhere.

"Where's what?" Mary Lou asked and knew by the fierce look on Doug's face that her question was out of order.

He opened and banged shut a couple more drawers, then swung to face Mary Lou. "My brothers have been in here, haven't they?"

"I don't know what you are talking about." Tom had told her under no circumstances to tell Doug that he and Zack had the extra set of keys. They had spent a lot of time just before Tom left looking for an important paper.

"You mean you, Tom, Zack, and my mother haven't been in here searching through these drawers while I'm gone? Don't give me that! I'm not dumb. I don't know how they do it but—"

The look of surprise on Mary Lou's face must have been a better answer than any words she could have conjured.

Doug continued to yank open and slam shut every drawer in the desk. When he found nothing, he reached into his vest pocket, took out the safe keys, and rummaged through the mess of papers inside with such vigor that they scattered all over the floor.

"What's going on here?"

The younger women stepped aside to let Allena enter.

Doug swung to his mother. "I thought I was supposed to run this ranch! I don't need any help from my brothers."

"This ranch belongs to all of us, Doug. We wonder why you don't let us share the burden of running it. It's too great a load for only one person."

Doug straightened up with a sneer. "Then help me find the land deed to the southeast corner. I must have that paper!"

Not quite knowing what the land deed looked like, all three women began sorting and folding papers into orderly piles.

Mary Lou shuddered. Chaos everywhere. The room even smelled stuffy and dusty. How could Doug know a deed was hidden in this mess of papers, let alone expect to find it?

No deed was found.

Doug shooed the women out of the office, locked it, grabbed Lily's hand, and hurried her back to their bedroom. Allena and Mary Lou turned toward the kitchen. Neither said a word.

"Will Mr. Doug be here for dinner? It's just about ready."

"I imagine so, Hattie. Mary Lou and I will set the table so we can eat before Doug goes back to town. He looks like he could stand a good meal. I wish he would take time to eat properly. He looks thinner every time I see him."

"No cookin' like home cookin'." Hattie went back to her pots.

In the past month, along with growing thinner, Doug had also become angrier and returned to his sullen ways. When he first brought Lily home, he had changed. He'd actually smiled and joked with his brothers. Lily's love had softened him.

On other days, Mary Lou didn't know how Lily put up with him. Yet, no matter what time of day or night Doug came home, Lily was there, checking to see if he had eaten or slept. She openly loved him and made him a good wife. He was lucky to have her. Mary Lou told her so. Lily blushed and bowed her head.

The dinner bell rang for the third time with impatience and volume. "Nothin' worse than cold food," Hattie mumbled and stomped back to the kitchen.

Everyone got her message and hurried to the table. The twins and baby Zack were bibbed and tied in chairs. In the barn, high chairs were in the process of being built.

Allena said grace and began passing dishes of food. "The ranch seems to be doing better," she said cheerfully. "Tom said we have at least a thousand more head going to market this year."

"He had better get top dollar. We need it." Doug ate hurriedly and glanced around. "Where's Nelson?"

"At Shepard's." Allena's face clouded.

Mary Lou knew Mother was troubled about Nelson and Laura. They spent a lot of time traveling back and forth between the Circle Z and the Bar-S. They were together as often as possible, open in their love for each other. Allena's only comment spoke to the neglect of Nelson's painting.

"Mother, I love my painting," Nelson had responded, "but I have to have something else. I need to be normal, or as normal as I can be. I want to marry Laura."

Oh, Lord, Mary Lou prayed, *help Allena to remember how she loved Father Zack and how necessary it is for Nelson to be joined to the one You have chosen for him. Let her listen to her heart, Lord, remembering how it was to be young and in love.*

Mary Lou had no doubt that if it hadn't been for God's intervention through Aunt Tibby and Aunt Nelda, she and Tom would have missed each other completely and been cheated out of the best.

If Allena didn't soften, it wouldn't surprise Mary Lou if Nelson and Laura took things in their own hands, especially with the Shepards on their side. Allena's heart would break if they moved without taking her into consideration—her fourth son to take matters into his own hands in the task of choosing his wife.

Mary Lou recognized the fear clutching Allena's heart. Fear for her baby. But Laura was right. Allena's little boy no longer existed. Nelson was a young man in love.

The women had only half-finished their meal when Doug shoved his empty plate away. "I've got to get back." He turned to Lily. "I'm staying in town tonight. See you tomorrow afternoon."

Lily followed him out.

Allena and Mary Lou fed bits of mashed food to the children. A smiling Lily returned to the table, picked up a spoon, and began feeding baby Zack. To nurse the twins, Mary Lou moved to the rocker.

Lily settled in the opposite rocking chair to give Baby Zack his bottle. When she finished, she took him outside for exercise and held his hands while the baby seriously maneuvered one high step after the other favoring one leg. Under Allena's tutelage, Lily's massage and exercise had encouraged baby Zack's short leg to grow a half inch, impressing Dr. Mike.

Sleepy children's faces washed, each woman rocked a baby until small eyelids drooped and closed. They tucked them quickly into bed for their naps and hurried to a waiting task.

Mary Lou gathered her curtain material and sewing implements into a basket, saddled Dulcie, and rode to their new house. She heard the rhythmic pounding of two hammers afar off. Tex and Bart had finished the floor in the bedroom and had moved the bed onto the spot she had told them, the small table and chair beside it.

A light, warm breeze skipped through the open door, exhaling a breath of cool air. Mary Lou settled to cut and sew. When finished, she stretched to the top of the window to tie the curtain cord to the nails on either side.

"Mighty pretty," Tex said as he stood at the door watching.

Mary Lou nodded. "Thank you. They should cheer up the place a bit, don't you think?" She pulled to wind the cord tighter around the nails on either side of the window. The curtains still sagged in the middle.

"Tex, could you pound me a nail in the middle so the curtains will hang straight across the top?"

"Yes ma'am." He pulled a nail from his pocket, poised it, and hammered. "How's that?"

"Perfect." Mary Lou stretched the cord, a panel on each side of the center nail. Then she and Tex anchored the cords to the frame on each side and stood back to appraise their work.

Tex hung back a moment. "Forgive me, ma'am, for sayin' so, but watchin' you and Tom makes me kinda hanker to find me a good woman I could make my missus." He rubbed his nose and grinned. "Trouble is, I can't seem to find a woman who will put up with me."

Mary Lou smiled. "It all depends on where you are looking. There are a lot of young women around these parts who are hunting for a good steady fellow like you."

Tex's eyebrows raise in surprise. "A cowboy?"

"What's wrong with a cowboy? My pa was one," Mary Lou's heart flew back to what Pa had been like when she was a little girl. He had sat solid in the saddle and laughed all the time. His accident had changed all that. Mary Lou bobbed her head.

"He was the best. My Aunt Tibby told me before I married Tom that cowboys were just young men doing a very hard job. She married Uncle Nate, who was a cowboy and now owns the biggest spread in Venture."

Mary Lou grinned. "She also said they make good husbands. So you see, there's hope for you." Mary Lou smiled at the red spots growing on Tex's cheeks. "Yep, someday you'll make some lucky girl a good husband, Tex, and I'll pray she'll come."

The color heightened. Tex ducked his head. "Thank ya, ma'am. I. . .uh. . .never heard anyone say it so good before."

Mary Lou gathered her materials into the basket. "But remember, if you want a good wife, you have to start looking in the right places." She laughed at the intrigued look on Tex's face. "Try church. We're going to build one soon. Maybe you'd like to help. Women and girls bring the noon meal."

Tex grinned and glowed.

"Lots of pretty ones, too. I'm sure you will find one that will take a shine to you. And more than likely she'd be a good cook. Things haven't changed much. The way to a man's heart. . . ." Mary Lou laughed, mounted Dulcie, and rode off, leaving Tex standing with his mouth open and some things to think about.

Trotting home, a sudden pain clutched Mary Lou's heart and brought with it new discovery. With Tom gone, she felt like only half a person and found herself looking for her other half wherever she went; at their new house, in the barn, she was constantly expecting her handsome, red-headed husband to walk through the door. She missed talking with him, sharing the amazing growth of the twins. Busy as she was, each day seemed like a month. The nights were forever.

Mary Lou often found herself gazing far into the horizon, hoping for a glimpse of Tom riding in on Tinder. Home for her had truly become wherever Tom was. She hungered for his embrace, the smother of his kisses, and his sweet whisperings of love. She would even enjoy the smell of hay, horses, and sweat that surrounded him when he rode hard through the Circle Z arch in a hurry to get home to see her and the twins.

Something Mama had said one night during one of their woman talks popped into her memory: "When you really love someone, they become so real and so much a part of you that you find if they are not near, part of you is gone." Mama had known. She had continued to love Pa even after the bitterness from his accident shoved his wife and daughter out of his life.

Mary Lou sighed. At least she was counting off the last days. If all went well, Tom could be home in two weeks. Another forever.

Supper chores done, babies asleep and tucked in, the women dragged their rockers outside. The wind cooled and calmed. Every so often a breeze fluttered by, touching everything. Descending twilight soothed the night with a covering of peace.

The women's chatter stalled. Their mouths at rest, they leaned their heads against the backs of their rockers, watching the sun close its eye and release its hold on the night.

Long after everyone had gone to bed, Mary Lou woke to the clamor of a horse's hooves. She sat up. Tom? She prepared to leap out of bed, but then sank back. Zack's voice? Then Allena's. Their muffled voices floated from. . .the office? Zack must have the keys.

Prickles in her neck filled Mary Lou with apprehension. Could something be wrong? Should she go and find out? With Tom not here. . . . She strained to listen. Abruptly the talking stopped, then continued outside. Suddenly, a horse snorted, stomped around, and took off in a gallop.

Mary Lou sat on the side of the bed, waiting to see if Allena would come. If it were something life-shaking, Allena surely would wake her. She waited in the quiet. Her shoulders slumped. It had been a tiring day. Her heavy eyelids refused to stay open. She gazed at the twins, motionless in their cradles. Mary Lou lay back and never remembered pulling up the cover.

sixteen

Breakfast over, Mary Lou tied a ribbon around her hair at the nape of her neck. An hour or so at the new house that morning and the curtains would be finished. Allena and Hattie had to hoe the vegetable garden, so Lily offered to care for all three babies.

By working together that evening, the four women would be able to finish the quilt. All it needed was the tying and it would be done before Tom got home. Mary Lou tucked her sewing basket handle into the crook of her arm and started for the barn. Tex usually had Dulcie all saddled and ready to go. Yep, he would make some lucky girl a good husband.

Halfway across the yard, Mary Lou stopped and watched an unfamiliar wagon roll slowly through the arch, Zack at the reins, Dr. Mike in the seat beside him. Two familiar saddled horses were tied behind. The looks on the men's faces shot panic into Mary Lou.

Tex, Bart, and the cowboys came out of the barn to gawk, then walked slowly to the hitching rail as the wagon bumped to a halt. Zack jumped off and walked into the house. He emerged shortly, his mother on one arm and Lily on the other.

Mary Lou's reluctant feet carried her to the wagon. Dr. Mike jumped down, and she followed him to the back. Last, Nelson came out of the house, moving as briskly as

143

he could.

Everyone gathered at the wagon, their eyes focused on a mound underneath the canvas. Mary Lou's heart held its breath. It looked like a. . . .

Dr. Mike folded back the canvas.

Allena gasped, her hands flew to her mouth. She broke from Zack's grasp and flung herself on the body of her son, sobs wrenching deep within. "No, no," she wailed. "Oh, Doug! Doug."

Lily stood transfixed, a look of utter disbelief on her face, her eyes wet and wild. Slowly she reached out and laid one hand on her mother-in-law's shoulder, the other on the leg of her husband.

Hattie rushed outside, looked into the wagon, and stepped back. She grabbed a corner of her apron to mop escaping tears, shook her head back and forth, and then voiced what everyone was thinking. "I knew it. I prayed, but I knew Mr. Doug was headin' fer no good end."

Mary Lou's gaze searched Zack, who looked haggard and drained. "What happened?"

"Let's go inside." Zack guided his mother, and Dr. Mike put his arm around Lily to steady her.

The cowboys rolled Doug's body in the canvas and carried it to his bedroom where they unrolled it onto the bed. Bart and Tex removed his boots.

"I'll finish," Allena said. "I'll wash and dress him." Her voice sounded hollow.

"Yes ma'am."

"I'll help." Lily held the door open for everyone to leave.

Hattie took back a basin of hot water, soap, and some

towels, and then left the two women who loved Doug most to do the last earthly thing they could do for him.

Hattie busied herself setting out spoons and cups which she filled with hot coffee. She pushed the sugar and cream in front of Dr. Mike. Before long, everyone but the two women were around the table. The cowboys stood behind, holding their steaming cups in their hands.

At first, no one talked. But the coffee revived their broken spirits, and Zack slowly began an explanation.

"Doug made another land sale. He received the money yesterday with a promise that he would turn over the land deed by supper time."

Mary Lou voiced her thoughts. "So that is why Doug was in such a frenzy in the ranch office yesterday!"

Zack nodded. "I saw him leave Harness in the afternoon and then come back. One of the sheriff's boys told me that they heard the land speculators were upset when the deed didn't arrive at supper time. They accused Doug of reneging on the deal. Doug told them he never kept important papers in town, so they insisted he go home last night. They followed him so he could get it and give it to them."

Then it was Doug, not Zack, Mary Lou had heard late so late at night!

Zack wet his dry mouth with a couple swallows of coffee. "The sheriff got wind of this deal last week. We planned to pretend we knew nothing, but we got ready for the speculators when they met Doug at supper time. Unfortunately what we didn't know was that Doug had already been given the money yesterday and had promised to have the deed by last night. That is why they followed him home to make sure they got the deed."

Unable to hide his moist eyes, Zack bowed his head. "What Doug didn't know was that I have it. Early this summer when I finally figured out what was going on, I took all the Circle Z deeds and put them in the safe in my office in town."

Nelson sat motionless, his eyes incensed. "You mean, they waited for Doug and shot him on his own land?"

Mary Lou could almost hear Nelson's thoughts. If he had been able, he would be out now riding wildly to find his brother's killers.

Zack said, "I don't know where he was shot. Somebody came running to my office this morning and told me my brother's horse with Doug's body tied over it had come to a halt behind the saloon. Dr. Mike declared him dead, and we brought him home." Zack drained his cup, pushed back his chair, and left for Doug's room.

Hattie sniffed loudly. "That poor boy never had a chance."

Hardly a boy, Mary Lou thought. She remembered Mama reading in Luke 12 about a foolish man who flaunts God. Jesus said, "But God said unto him, Thou fool, this night thy soul shall be required of thee: then whose shall those things be, which thou hast provided?"

Zack stood in the doorway. "He's ready now."

After the family left, the cowboys stood about uneasy. Hattie went around with the coffee pot again. Shortly, Zack came back.

"You can go in now." His voice broke. He cleared his throat and gulped a couple swallows of coffee. Zack's nostrils flared, his jaws flexed. "They shot him in the back."

The cowboys stiffened. Silence enveloped the room like a shroud. It was one thing for a man to be shot facing his enemy, another to be shot from behind without a chance. Even a scoundrel didn't deserve that.

Later the barn resounded with hammers pounding nails into boards to make Doug's burying box.

Emily Shepard stayed close to Allena, who sat unnaturally quiet in one of the rocking chairs beside the fireplace.

The next day, wagons from neighbors filled the yard. They brought all kinds of food and comfort. Doug was laid in his burying box on two sawhorses in the parlor. One by one, the neighbors paid their respects.

Emily Shepard stayed close to Allena, sensing her needs.

Someone came from town and said Pastor Clayburn had been notified and would be at the burying early in the afternoon as soon as he could travel to Harness.

Mary Lou ached for Tom. Doug's death would be a greater shock when he came back than if he had been here. Now they were surrounded with loving support from neighbors and friends. Tom would have to take the loss square on the chin.

The wooden box holding Doug was already on the wagon when Pastor Clayburn came. Other wagons and neighbors on horseback followed the family to the Langdon cemetery.

Zack, Tex, Bart, and Will Shepard, with Nelson following on his crutches, carried the box with Doug's body to the fresh grave in the family cemetery and lowered it in with ropes. A damp wind blew a hint of rain, creating a sense of urgency.

Everyone gathered around the open grave. Women, dressed in black, stood close to their husbands. Timid, wide-eyed children shied into their mother's wide skirts.

Pastor Clayburn opened his Bible. "Let not your heart be troubled. . . ."

Did every pastor begin a funeral service with the same words? Mary Lou's heart pounded and her memory rushed her back to another fall day when she had stared down into the grave holding her mother. The vacuum returned and revived her complete sense of loss. Tears streamed down her face. She was ashamed to admit they were not for Doug.

She gazed at Allena. Was she reliving the day she had laid her husband in the next grave?

"And those who believe in the Lord Jesus Christ and live according to His Word will live again. That is God's promise."

A heaviness settled on Mary Lou. As far as she knew or could discern, Doug had never accepted Jesus Christ. She remembered Tom one time saying that when they were little, his father had been firm about them accepting Christ as Savior. Had Doug taken that step as a small boy? A young man?

Yet, how did anyone truly know if someone had accepted Jesus as Lord and Savior? Mama had always said that that was between a person and God, but that we were to love people regardless, like God loves us. But if Doug had not. . . .

Mary Lou gazed at Allena and shared her grief. Whether Doug was guilty or not, Allena grieved for her son. Did

God grieve for his lost ones, too?

"And may God have mercy on his soul." Pastor Clayburn closed his Bible and walked to Allena's side. A restless hush followed.

Zack stepped forward and picked up the first shovel. He pushed it into the soft earth and slowly tipped it.

The sound of the dirt hitting the box exploded in Mary Lou's brain. *Mama!* Her soul cried out in the pain of remembering. She felt alone and ached for Tom's comforting arms. Slowly an unexplainable warmth enveloped her, and she rested in a wash of reassurance that death was never the end.

Allena reached for a handful of dirt and poured it slowly through her fingers into the grave. Zack handed the shovel to Nelson and stepped behind him to balance him. Allena reached for his crutches. Nelson filled the shovel with dirt and poured it into the grave. He turned to Lily and stretched forth the shovel.

Lily drew back a moment, but after a smile of encouragement from Allena, she filled the shovel. With dry, sad eyes, she slowly poured the soil into the grave.

Everyone stood silently. Zack put his arm around his mother's shoulders, took Lily's hand, and led them both to the buggy. Nelson followed and climbed in the driver's seat. The buggy pulled away, and Zack returned to join his neighbors.

The dirt clods fell softer and softer as Zack and his neighbors dropped each shovelful into the grave.

For the first time in his life, Douglas Langdon was at rest.

seventeen

Doug's death hung a pall over the ranch.

Allena worked constantly, quietly, the strain of the loss of one of her sons mirrored in her grief-stricken eyes.

Lily seemed to be in a daze but faithfully did her chores, her sweet smile reduced to a small line across pale lips. She left the ranch every morning, walking no one knew where, but always returned before baby Zack woke. When not doing chores, she cared for the baby and couldn't hide her obvious love for him. He was the only one who could call a smile to her face.

Every morning as soon as chores were done, Allena gathered Mary Lou, Lily, and Hattie into the parlor for devotions. They searched the Bible for words of comfort they found nowhere else.

Emily and Laura Shepard came often to join them. Emily also knew the heartbreak of losing a son. Her little Timothy had been three when he had wandered into the path of an angry bull who gored and killed him.

Gradually the overriding undercurrent concerning the marriage of Nelson and Laura surfaced. At first, it was a comment here and there. One morning it blossomed into a full-blown discussion.

"I'd like to know your objections, Allena. Laura is brokenhearted." Emily's face was firm, her eyes pained.

"Emily, we have always talked plain to each other. I

love Laura and consider her as my own."

"I know that, which makes it more difficult to understand your hesitancy about Nelson and Laura's marriage."

"You know the responsibility a man takes on when he marries. Under God, he vows to care of his wife and...." Allena paused.

Emily finished, "And for any children they may have? Is that what bothers you?"

Allena's disturbed gaze searched Emily, then the other women. "Well, yes. I'm concerned about that, but the largest part of a man's job is to provide for his own."

"My dear friend, as Laura's mother I am naturally concerned that any young man my daughter would choose to marry would have the ability to take care of her. But I have no doubt Nelson can do that, and neither does Laura.

"Allena, you should see him work with the cowboys at our ranch. Sometimes it is hard for them to remember there is anything wrong with him. He finds his own way to handle any situation. He and Laura work together like a well-matched team of horses."

Emily shook her head. "Allena. Think back. Remember what it was like when you and Zack met and fell in love. Nelson and Laura love each other and want to get married, and no reason you have given is more important than that."

Baby cries voiced a need. Hattie and Lily rose quickly and waved their hands at Mary Lou to stay put, then slipped out quietly.

In the trapped look upon her mother-in-law's face, Mary Lou could almost read her thoughts. Shortly after Mary Lou came to Texas, Allena had told her, "When Zack died, I transferred my love to my boys." Must she desperately hang on to them to give her life meaning?

Mary Lou knew it had hurt Allena to have been left out when Zack, Tom, and Doug had chosen their wives. Was Allena grasping Nelson as her last straw?

But that was not the way love worked. Mama had said love multiplies when you give it away. Was Allena blinded to the fact that she could drive a permanent wedge between herself and Nelson if she kept him from marrying the woman he loved?

Nelson and Laura walked into the parlor. "Since you are all talking about us, don't you think it would be well if you asked us how we feel?" Nelson asked.

Looks of startled guilt crossed faces and tied tongues.

"Mother, I know you want me to be happy. You've given me full proof of that all my life. You taught me not to feel like a cripple, that I can accomplish what I want to do in spite of my legs. But I have never thought of myself as a cripple—until now. That seems to be the only thing keeping Laura and me from being married. Mother, I love Laura, but if there is some other girl you think would make me a better wife, tell me who." Nelson's voice was quiet, controlled.

Allena bowed her head.

The room waited impatiently.

When Allena raised her head to Nelson's anxious face, her eyes swam with tears, but she was smiling. "Thank you, Nelson, for asking." She kissed his cheek. "You are the first son to ask me that. You've grown into a man before my very eyes, but I refused to acknowledge it."

She stood up, walked to her son, and held his face between her hands. "In truth, I am the cripple. Since your father died I've leaned hard on four strong crutches. It's time I stood up and learned to walk on my own."

Nelson started to say something, but she put her hand over his mouth.

"Let me finish. Zack told me it was time I recognized the fact that my boys are men." She turned to Laura and kissed her, took both her hands, and gave them to Nelson. "Of all the girls in the world, Laura is the only one I would choose for your wife because I know she loves you. After loving and being loved by your father, that's what I want for you."

Laura and Nelson grabbed Allena at the same time and squeezed her.

"Wait a minute," Allena gasped. "You haven't heard my one condition."

Nelson beamed. "Anything, mother."

"That you live here at the Circle Z. Tom and Mary Lou will be moving into their own place." She paused with a sigh. "Doug's gone, and the few of us who are left are going to rattle around this ranch and get lost if you don't."

Leaning firmly on one crutch, his arm around her, Nelson gazed into Laura's eyes. Whatever communication passed between them escaped the onlookers. They turned to Allena with two wide smiles. "That suits us fine, providing we can be married next Saturday." Nelson grabbed Laura and kissed her in front of everybody.

The tension in the room lifted and bounced away on everyone's laughter.

Busy days followed. As requested, the wedding would take place at the Bar-B ranch at twelve o'clock. Zack told Dr. Mike, which was as good as handing the news to the Pony Express. Trips were made back and forth between the two ranches. Laura's belongings began to arrive at the Circle Z, and the women scurried to find space for them in Nelson's room. Laura insisted in leaving Nelson's easel by the window for his painting. The stacks of pictures that controlled the floor space were hung everywhere. Even in the kitchen. Nelson painted Hattie making bread.

Toward the end of the week, tantalizing aromas wafted from the kitchen. Hattie outdid herself with a huge wedding cake filled with dried fruit and nuts.

Mary Lou thanked God for answering her prayer for Nelson and Laura and joined eagerly with preparations. Yet, even amid the flurry, her constant thought was of Tom's return. She hourly searched the horizon for his familiar shape moving along in the rhythm of an easy gait astride Tinder. She rose early one day, sensing a deep feeling within that he could come at any moment.

Tex and Bart had loaded Mama's dresser, chest, and rocking chairs in the wagon, each wrapped in quilts for protection, and were ready to move them to the new house. They criss-crossed rope on the bottom of the bed to hold the mattress bag Mary Lou had made out of rough ticking fabric stuffed as firmly as she could with straw and hay. She had stuffed the under side with a layer of goose feathers so she could flop it come winter. That way, the straw would be cooler in summer, the feathers would create warmth for winter. When she could afford muslin for sheets, she would make some. For now, they would sleep between Mama's quilts.

Mary Lou smiled as the cowboys unloaded the wagon. Tucked in a large wash basin were soap and lots of flour sacks for use as dish towels, diapers, cleaning cloths, or whatever, a contribution from Hattie.

The gardens around the ranch house had grown an abundance of vegetables. The women picked almost daily. Those vegetables which could not be eaten were put into flour sacks and stored in the root cellars.

Mary Lou thanked Hattie for generously donating some of the ranch vegetables to her new home. She opened the trap door in the kitchen floor and climbed down the ladder into her new root cellar. She stacked her first vegetable bags side by side on the dirt ledge the men had carved out of the wall.

In the bedroom, she spread the quilts over the mattress, put the wash basin on the dresser with Mama's pitcher, spread a new rug on each side of the bed, and then stood back to appraise her work. Beautiful! Her heart swelled with pride. Everything was ready for Tom, whenever he came. She sighed, praying it would be soon.

"Is this the new home of Mr. and Mrs. Thomas Langdon?"

"Tom!" Mary Lou spun around and flew out of the bedroom into the arms of her husband. As his mouth pressed hungrily on hers, Mary Lou's heart pounded dizzily. She clung to Tom, relishing the feel of his body next to hers as the tight enclosure of his arms melted them together and made her feel whole again. Tom was home!

Tom slowly released her and stretched her to arm's length. His gaze roamed every inch. "I couldn't stand another day. I left Smitty and the boys yesterday and rode all night." He gathered Mary Lou into his arms, gentler this time, and touched his lips to hers again and again, drinking in their soft sweetness.

When he released her, he stepped behind her, closed his

arms around her, and surveyed the room. "I can't believe it. You have done wonders to this place."

Mary Lou wiggled from his arms and grabbed his hand. "Come see." She pulled him to the bedroom.

He turned an inquiring gaze from the bedroom to Mary Lou and lifted the quilts and the mattress. "Who roped it?"

"Tex. He has been a great help. In fact, this has set him thinking that maybe he ought to find himself a wife."

Tom laughed. "Wait a minute. He is too good a man to lose." His arms encircled Mary Lou again. "But I wouldn't want to deprive a man of a wife. Hope he finds a good one like I have." He kissed her soundly. "Now I would wish that on any man."

They walked into the twins' bedroom. Mary Lou had had Tex build beds right on the walls of the room. Instead of rope, Tex had constructed a solid bottom, making a box which Mary Lou filled with straw and hay. She covered the filling with ticking fabric until she could make mattress bags. In a week, Tommy and Beth would be four months old. Before long, they would learn to sit. Their cradles would be too small.

Mary Lou hugged Tom again. "Have you any idea how glad I am you are home? I missed you."

"Me too." Tom pulled her into his arms and held her.

Tinder and Dulcie nickered outside.

"Poor Tinder. I rode him hard. He needs feed and a good rest." Tom kissed Mary Lou again and pulled her toward the door. "Time to get back to the ranch."

Mary Lou didn't tell Tom about Doug. He needed to enjoy his homecoming. Zack should be the one to tell him.

Zack had just walked into the ranch kitchen with baby

Zack when Tom and Mary Lou opened the kitchen door. He stretched out his hand and smiled a welcome. "Welcome home. How was the trip?"

Tom grabbed his brother's hand. "Too long."

Zack laughed. "Makes a difference to have a family at home, doesn't it?" Zack frowned. "I didn't hear Smitty and the boys come in."

"They'll be here tomorrow. I left them at Doan's crossing."

Lily entered the kitchen, the twins in her arms.

Tom gazed with delight, took them into his arms, and stared in amazement. "I can't believe how they have grown."

Everyone laughed.

Hattie, a platter of steak in one hand and a bowl of creamed potatoes and onions in the other, nodded. "Babies do that," she said and disappeared into the dining room.

Tom dried his hands on the towel and his mother walked into the kitchen.

"Oh, Tom." She embraced him, clung, and sobbed.

Taken by surprise Tom looked from one member of the family to the other. Then Zack told him of Doug's death.

As Tom listened, his jaw tightened and a look of fury spread across his face. "And nobody has any idea of who did it?"

"I'm sure somebody knows, but they are going to make sure I never find out."

"Dinner's getting cold." Hattie stated flatly.

The family ate and talked until the twins and baby Zack grew restless tied in their chairs. Mary Lou and Lily untied them and took them to the kitchen to feed them their milk.

After the babies were fed, Hattie took Tommy and Beth from Mary Lou. "You and Tom just ride up to your house and leave these babies with me. I'm afraid they'll fall out of those new beds."

Bless Hattie, Mary Lou thought with a smile at her candor.

Tom came out shortly, nodded at the arrangement, and kissed and held his son and daughter again.

They began their walk to their new home. On their way, they stopped at the cemetery and stood beside Doug's fresh grave.

"Strange. At this moment, I cannot think of a thing I have against my brother, even though I have had an inner dislike of him all my life and hated myself for it. As a Christian, I felt I should love him in spite of everything. I admit it was hard!"

"You did love him, Tom. And he loved you and Zack and Nelson and his mother as best he could. Like my pa. Mama said he still had love in his heart, but his accident made him so angry he refused to let it out, pushed us from him, and threw his life away. Doug did too.

"My real sorrow for him is that he denied himself so much by acting as he did. He baited people to hurt them and got hurt in return and wondered why. The way he talked to Lily and treated her. . . ." Mary Lou shook her head. "But it is over. Now he is in God's hands, and we must forget the unpleasant memories or they will sour us. That will be our fault."

They reached their door, stood with their arms around each other, and looked up. The heavens radiated peace as myriads of tiny lights poked holes through the dense blue night sky to wink and blink at the world and soothe its spirit.

They opened the door. A whole new life stood on tiptoe before them. Tom lit a lamp. Eerie shadows danced on the walls as they undressed for bed.

Tom extinguished the lamp, and they climbed into bed. A satisfying contentment settled on Mary Lou. She turned to her husband's arms. Tom was home. So was she.

eighteen

Laura, dressed in blue, stepped out of the ranch door on Will Shepard's arm.

Her father led her between neighbors and friends standing by a group of beech trees decked in golden leafy gowns. He placed Laura beside Nelson. Her smile radiated joy as her sparkling eyes rested on Nelson. She held a bouquet of flowers in one arm and placed her other hand over Nelson's on his crutch.

Tom and Mary Lou took places beside them.

Pastor Clayburn cleared his throat, looked out over the assembly, and opened his Bible.

Gazing at Laura's happy face triggered the memory of the happiness Mary Lou had felt as Pa walked her through Aunt Tibby's parlor to Glenn's side. Now even thinking about it churned her stomach. Glenn's rejection of her at the altar was the most humiliating experience of her life, but she blessed him for it. It had opened the door for Tom to be her husband.

Pastor Clayburn cleared his throat. "Friends and neighbors, we are gathered together to join in holy matrimony Nelson Langdon and Laura Shepard. If there is anyone who objects to this union, speak now or forever hold your peace."

Mary Lou held her breath. Her own wedding had fallen apart after those words.

The pastor turned to Nelson. "Do you, Nelson Langdon,. . . ."

Mary Lou could not see Nelson's face, but his answer vibrated with joy. In a few moments, his dream would come to reality.

"And do you, Laura Shepard, take Nelson Langdon to be your lawfully wedded husband, to cherish, honor, and obey him and keep yourself only unto him? If so, say I do."

"I do." Laura's gaze never left Nelson's beaming face.

"In the name of the Father, Son, and Holy Ghost, I pronounce you man and wife. Beware you let no man set you asunder." He gazed out over the people gathered. "Let us pray." He bowed his head.

"Father in heaven, in Your Word, You made the woman out of the rib of a man and joined them together. Let these two, standing before us today, be joined together by hearts of love in Jesus Christ. Amen." He turned to the newlyweds. "God bless you, my children."

Laura turned to Nelson, put her arms around him, and they sealed their vows with a kiss. Then they turned into a circle of friends who expressed good wishes and pressed presents into their hands.

To Texans, any social event, be it wedding or funeral, was an occasion to bring people together from miles around. Daily existence was monotonous, so any opportunity to meet with their neighbors became cherished time.

Will Shepard stepped in front of the food table and raised his hand. "Friends, the ladies have outdone themselves making all this good food. Eat your fill to give you strength to continue our celebration at the barn dance. Now it's time to thank the good Lord for His blessings."

He bowed his head.

Hats came off. All heads bowed.

"Our Father, we ask Your blessing not only on our food, but also upon the marriage of Laura and Nelson. We thank You for good neighbors and friends to join us at this happy time. In Jesus' name, Amen."

Along the shady side of the house, long tables made from boards put on top of barrels groaned under the weight of roast beef and antelope, wild turkey, and all the special dishes from the guests' gardens and kitchens. One table alone proved too small for the wedding cake and all the pumpkin and apple pies, bread pudding, fat loaves of bread, and fancy jams, so two more barrels and boards were hastily assembled.

Hattie's wedding cake was delicious. It didn't last very long. Mary Lou watched her cut a small piece and put it into her basket. She caught Hattie's eye and wiggled her finger at her.

Hattie shook her head. "'Taint for me. I'm taking it home to put under Lily's pillow. I'm worried about her. Since Doug's death, she's a different girl. Maybe this will help bring her another husband to cheer her up."

Mary Lou smiled at Hattie's solution to Lily's problem, but she, too, had been concerned about her sister-in-law. She gazed over the crowd. Poor Lily. Claretta Pearson had her cornered and was enumerating her ailments and the woes of living in this forsaken country. Claretta came from Virginia and it was all she ever talked about. Mary Lou hurried to rescue Lily.

When the guests had eaten their fill, Alvin Yeager, the fiddler, began to saw his fiddle and call for dancers. Toes tapped and feet shuffled till the dancers found their partners for five rounds of the Virginia reel. To give them a rest, Alvin played a half-dozen waltzes, and Tom led off dancing with the bride. His big feet and long legs stayed miraculously unentangled and in rhythm.

Then stomp! Stomp! Stomp! Stomp! Alvin changed the tempo, called for squares, and his fiddle screeched "Turkey in the Straw." Ladies and gentlemen formed squares, and in obedience to Alvin's calls, skirts swung wide, feet shuffled, and the square dancers bounced in time to clapping onlookers.

What fun!

The twins and baby Zack got passed from arms to laps, as did other small babies, to allow their mothers freedom to join the merriment.

The stalwart sun presided over the day until a bright, silver moon rose to take its place and remind the guests it was time to board their wagons, buggies, and horses and head for home.

The bride and groom climbed into a new buggy given to them for a wedding present and, midst waves and shouts, left for Tom and Mary Lou's new house to stay for a two-day honeymoon, Mary Lou and Tom's gift to the newlyweds.

Mary Lou thought of the gift when she remembered the precious days she and Tom had spent alone together on their trip from Kansas to Texas. By the time they reached Texas, they were truly man and wife.

Riding back in the wagon to the Circle Z where Tom, Mary Lou, and the twins would stay for the two days the newlyweds were at their home, she breathed a silent prayer of thanks for the blessing of God's gift of marriage. Never had she been happier. She glanced down at the two tired, sleeping children in her arms, then at the young man beside her who loved her and made life worth living. Never in all her cottonwood dreams could she have imagined such happiness.

The next morning, Mary Lou struggled to open her eyes. She reached for Tom. He was gone. She raised up on her elbow to check the twins. They were gone, too.

Mary Lou took the luxury of lying back down for a few minutes. The past weeks of working on the house and the work of the wedding had added up to exhaustion. Her legs refused to swing over the edge of the bed. She dozed off. When her eyelids opened again, sunlight had captured the whole room.

Mary Lou threw back the covers and sat up. The house was unusually quiet. What time was it? Without Tom's pocket watch, she had no way of knowing, but it had to be late. The sun was high.

Energy triggered within. She should be up and about! Hattie and Allena planned to get the meat hanging in the barn ready for drying. She hurried and dressed.

When Mary Lou opened the kitchen door, Hattie grinned.

"Did you get your beauty sleep?"

Mary Lou laughed. "I don't know whether I got it or not. I slept too hard to find out." She looked around. "Where are Tommy and Beth?"

"With Miz Langdon. She has all three."

"Where's Lily?" Mary Lou grinned. "Did you put the cake under her pillow?"

"I didn't have a chance. It was too late. She went to bed

before I could do it." Hattie's brows knit together. "I'm a bit concerned. Lily isn't back from her walk yet."

"When did she leave?"

"As soon as she fed baby Zack his breakfast and exercised his leg."

Mary Lou glanced outside. "It's a beautiful day. I don't blame her. I would like to go out myself and just wander. Yesterday was a big day."

Hattie's face remained troubled.

Mary Lou touched her cheek and smiled. "A little prayer might not hurt if you're so concerned. Did Allena have morning devotions yet?"

"No, she said we would wait for you."

Mary Lou went to the parlor. They were all there. Baby Zack wobbled on two hands and two knees, but nothing seemed to work together well enough to gain any ground. The twins, on their backs on a blanket, had their four arms and legs flying. Tommy threw one leg over the other, turning him on his side. One of these days, Mary Lou expected to find him over on his stomach.

"Good morning. Have you had morning devotions yet?"

"No, I have been waiting for you and Lily. Her daily walks get longer and longer. I believe she is grieving for Doug."

Mary Lou nodded. "I've noticed that. The only one who seems to give her any happiness is baby Zack."

Hattie came in. They decided not to wait for Lily. Allena read aloud from the book of First John.

Beth grew fussy, so Mary Lou nursed her while Allena read Scripture. Beth soon fell asleep in her arms. Allena made a little bed on the floor in the corner with blankets, laid Beth in it, and then continued her reading. Then Mary Lou nursed Tommy, and shortly his eyes grew drowsy and closed. They put him in the other corner and covered both babies.

Devotions over, Allena picked up baby Zack, and the three women tiptoed out. They went from room to room, gathering dirty clothes to take out to the wash tubs to soak.

Hattie came flying out of Lily's room. "Miz Langdon, come quick!"

Was Lily sick? Had she come back from her walk and gone to her room without them noticing her?

Lily's room was neat, orderly, and empty.

Too orderly, Mary Lou thought. Her dresses were not hanging on the wall pegs and her comb and brush were gone from beside the basin.

"She's gone!" Hattie looked from Allena to Mary Lou. "All her stuff is gone!"

It was true. Mary Lou found the two calico dresses she had given her laying on her bed.

Hattie stayed with the babies while Allena and Mary Lou started out to find the missing girl. They went to the barn. The cowboys said Lily hadn't come for a horse. Tom and Smitty had ridden out on the range right after breakfast. It was a fruitless search. Lily was nowhere on the ranch.

As they returned to the house, Allena voiced her thoughts. "I'm afraid to say what I think, but she must have gone back to Harness." Allena sadly shook her head, her eyes clouded.

"Where would she go?" Mary Lou asked.

Allena bowed her head and said, "Probably back to

where she came from. Where else could she go?"

Mary Lou shook her head. "No! I won't think that of Lily. She's a sweet girl."

"I agree with you. I admit I was shocked when Doug brought her home, but after I got to know her and learned she had been orphaned at ten and raised in an orphanage until she was sixteen, I understood that the poor girl just got swallowed up in circumstances."

Mary Lou's heart ached too much to say anything. She did not believe Lily would go back to the brothel. How could she? Not after that morning when she had accepted Jesus as her Savior and was so repentant.

Suddenly Allena was on the move. "Put on your bonnet, Mary Lou. We are going to town."

nineteen

Allena and Mary Lou got to Harness about noon and parked in front of the saloon. Ignoring raised eyebrows and questioning looks, they climbed out of the buggy and walked through the front door.

The nauseating odor of whisky assaulted Mary Lou's nostrils and reminded her of the day the women of Venture went into Mac Ludden's saloon with hatchets and axes. Now she felt the same incensed anger. If an ax had been at the end of her arm, she would have smashed it through the front window the same as she had in Kansas.

Bleary-eyed, cocky men and shameless, gaudy women stared. Allena, head high with all the dignity of a matriarch, marched boldly to the highly polished oak bar. "Could you tell me, please, is Lily Langdon here?"

The barkeep lifted his eyebrows. "Lily Lang—? Why, uh. . .no, ma'am. I ain't seen her since she. . .uh. . . ."

"Thank you." Allena didn't wait for him to finish. She turned and walked decisively toward the stairs. Mary Lou caught her breath, hesitated, then followed.

A dark-haired girl with large, penetrating brown eyes standing halfway up the stairs walked down to meet Allena and shook her head. "You don't want to go up there, ma'am. Lily isn't there."

Allena stared into her soul. "How do I know you are telling the truth?"

A wistful smile softened the girl's face. "I know Lily well, and I am telling you the truth. She isn't here. She never really belonged here."

A painted girl, hand on hip, sidled toward Allena and stood in front of her. "She married your son, ma'am. I knew him well." Her lip curled into a sneer. Her gaze scanned the room and returned to rest on Allena. "Or didn't he bring her home?"

Allena never flinched. "Yes, he did, on the same day he married her, which makes Lily my daughter-in-law. I want no harm to come to her."

The girl raised her eyebrows and shrugged her shoulders.

During Allena's encounter, Mary Lou viewed the other girls. Some stood brazenly at the bar, others draped themselves over men as they sat at cards, one plunked herself into a man's lap. But they all had one thing in common. Sad, veiled eyes. Lily had had those eyes when she first came home with Doug. It took baby Zack to rip the veil away and reveal the deep well of love that Lily had kept locked out of sight.

"Thank you and good-day," Mary Lou heard Allena say. She followed her out the door, shutting it on the howl of laughter.

Once outside, they noticed Dr. Mike coming out of the boarding house on the way to his buggy. He waved, leaned on a hitching post, and waited. He tipped his hat. "Good morning, Allena, Mary Lou. What brings you to town?"

"I'm looking for Lily."

Dr. Mike's eyes narrowed. "Something wrong?"

"She hasn't been herself since Doug died. This morning

we found she had packed her clothes and left."

Dr. Mike pursed his lips. "Hmm. I'm sure there is some good reason."

"What reason is good enough to leave your family?"

"Maybe Lily doesn't feel like your family since Doug is gone, or the ranch reminds her too much of Doug and she thought it would be better if she got away. There are lots of reasons, Allena, some of which none of us would understand."

"Well, if in your travels you find out anything, please let me know. If you see her, tell her I still consider her my daughter-in-law. We love her, Baby Zack cries for her, and I would like her to come home where she belongs."

Dr. Mike smiled and nodded. "I'll tell her just that if I see her, and if she will come with me, I will bring her out." He tipped his hat. "Good-day, ladies."

Allena and Mary Lou both tipped their heads, said good-day, and crossed the dusty street to the general store. "Might as well get a few things since we're here. We always need more sugar, flour, and salt. And you need muslin for sheets."

As they entered Orval Picket's Mercantile, Mary Lou felt a twang of homesickness. In the center was the pot-bellied stove, chairs around it and a cuspidor beside it. Other than the placement of supplies, general stores were much the same. The back wall was lined with barrels and tubs containing pickles, tobacco, crackers, sugar, flour, and who knew what else. Above them, shelves climbed to the ceiling trying to supply everything anyone asked for. Built-in bins contained coffee, tea, dried peas, fruit, rice, and oatmeal.

Mary Lou sniffed. There must be spice drawers nearby. The aroma of pepper, cinnamon, cloves, and other spices permeated the air. She closed her eyes and breathed deeply. The sounds and smells transported Mary Lou back to her father's store in Kansas.

Along a side wall stood four iron cookstoves. She walked over to one and ran her hand over the hard, black surface. She could picture it sitting in her new kitchen. What luxury it would be to be able to set pans of food on top of the stove to cook instead of standing in front of a hot fireplace on a summer's day stirring a pot hanging on the swingarm. She opened the oven door. Oh, to be able to bake bread in an oven like this. Someday. . . .

With the help of one of the young boys in the store, they carried their purchases to the buggy and climbed in.

Allena picked up the reins but didn't move. "I feel as if there is somewhere else we should ask questions."

"What about the boarding house? Lily will have to stay some place."

"Dr. Mike surely would have said something."

"Maybe she is there but he didn't see her. He is gone a lot."

They climbed back out of the buggy and went down the street to Jenny Wagner's boarding house.

"Yes, she was here trying to find a job, but I don't need any more cooks or house maids," Jenny told them.

"Did she say where she might be going?" Mary Lou asked.

Jenny slowly shook her head. "No, she just looked real sad and left. I felt sorry for her, but there was nothing I could do except offer her a meal, which she refused."

Allena turned to go, then hesitated. "Jenny, do me a favor."

"Yes'm?"

"I would appreciate it—if you see Lily or hear anything about her—if you would tell Dr. Mike so he could get word to me. If she comes back again or you see her anywhere, offer her a job, any job, then let me know. I'll come and get her and repay you any money you have paid her."

Jenny lowered her head and stood uneasy. "Pardon me, ma'am, for saying so, but...did you...did you check...uh, the saloon? Upstairs?"

Allena pulled herself to her full height and looked Jenny straight in the eye. "Yes, I did. She has not been there. She is not that kind of girl anymore. She is my daughter-in-law and a Christian."

Jenny's face registered shocked surprise. "Oh, yes, ma'am. If I see her, I'll do as you say, Mrs. Langdon."

Allena walked from the boarding house with all the poise and dignity of a true lady. Like Mama.

Buttons seemed to take his time on the way home. It didn't matter. Mary Lou and Allena were absorbed in their own thoughts.

Mary Lou was praying for Lily's safety and had no doubt her mother-in-law was doing the same. Things were different for Lily now; she belonged to God. That was it! She was God's child. He would protect her. Mary Lou's prayers turned into praise rather than worried pleas, thankful for all He had done for Lily already. She even praised God for Doug bringing Lily out of a life of ill repute. For the first time, Mary Lou prayed with a proper attitude for Doug. Without realizing it, he had done a good thing.

It was almost supper time when the buggy turned under the Circle-Z arch. Hattie came out the door and peered under her hand, searching to see if Lily was with them. When the buggy stopped, she shook her head. "You didn't find her?"

"No." Allena climbed out of the buggy.

Hattie raised her eyes. "Oh, God, take care of our Lily."

In the days that followed, the family noticed a change in baby Zack. He was restless, didn't sleep well, and cried a lot.

"Is he sick?" Zack asked his mother one night when nothing seemed to settle him.

"No. I think he misses Lily."

Zack sat and stared into the fireplace. "He needs his mother to come home."

"Did Darcy say anything about coming home in the letter you received the other day?"

"She said she would like to stay and celebrate Christmas with her family once more."

Mary Lou could tell by the set of Zack's jaw that Darcy being away so long bothered him. Over two months. In every letter Zack received, Darcy wrote of some special reason for her to stay: her mother's birthday, her best friend's marriage, her father's illness.

"Maybe he misses the twins since we moved. Maybe if we took him home with us to be with the twins. . . ." Mary Lou offered.

Zack turned pained eyes to Mary Lou. "It might help. The poor little fellow is deserted."

Laura and Nelson walked in and surprised everyone.

Contentment shone on two happy faces. "What little fellow is deserted?" Laura asked. "Baby Zack? Where's Lily?"

Mary Lou and Allena told of their visit to Harness.

"I'll be glad to help take care of him."

Mary Lou laughed, "Thanks, Laura. Two is trouble but three. . . ."

"Is one too many at any age," Allena added.

Long after everyone had gone to bed, Zack and Tom sat in front of the fireplace talking about the ranch and the changes to be made now that they would run it together.

Two of the deeds written up for land deals were not legal, so Doug's debts were not honored.

"By law," Zack said, "after a man is dead, his family is not liable for his gambling debts."

In practice, anyone who didn't pay a gambling debt might have to pay for it later with his life. And both brothers knew it.

twenty

Allena lifted baby Zack out of the wooden tub of bath water, wrapped him in a blanket, and laid him on his back on the kitchen table. His lips puckered, then opened to make way for a protesting scream.

Left in the tub, Tommy and Beth squealed with delight, banged their hands on the surface of the water, and soaked Mary Lou, Laura, and the floor. They joined baby Zack on the kitchen table to be dried and dressed.

Allena massaged her grandson's little legs straight, held them together, and smiled. "I do believe the short leg is growing."

She sat the baby on his bottom, measured his legs in a sitting position, grinned, and gave him a bear hug. "One of these days, dear baby, you will run like the wind." She kissed the top of his head.

"Since you massage his legs four times a day, Mother, show me how to do it. I could do it a couple times and give you a rest."

"Thank you, Laura. It is really very simple." Allena laid baby Zack on his back and worked her fingers in kneading fashion up and down along his whole leg into his back. He quieted as soon as her hands touched him.

"Knead gently, but firmly to stimulate the blood to come into his legs, Dr. Mike says. Then rub your hands up and down his leg, around his legs, and massage his little feet.

Press your fingers gently under each toe and rub so the toe stands at attention. Then do it again, several times. He'll fuss when he has had enough."

Laura shook her head in amazement. "Where did you learn how to do this? Who taught you?"

"God." Allena smiled at Laura's skeptical expression. "Desperate mothers try desperate measures. I figured if God made our bodies, as the Good Book says, then He certainly would tell us how to take care of them. Dr. Mike was very interested in what I was doing. Now he says if I hadn't worked with Nelson's legs, the muscles would have shriveled and Nelson would have been confined to a chair. At least he's mobile."

Mary Lou dried the sturdy, kicking legs of Tommy and praised God for His blessings.

"Then one day," Allena continued, "when Nelson was about three, my Zack came in from the barn carrying a tiny set of crutches he had made and taught Nelson to use them. Nelson, delighted, worked and struggled, falling more often than walking. Some days it broke my heart to watched him struggle to drag one foot after the other between those crutches. But his little heart was bigger and more determined than my faith.

"To our amazement, he finally mastered them by placing a crutch as a balance beside one leg, then swinging the balance from one leg and crutch to the other, strengthening his shoulders and arms as well. He may not walk as you or I, but he gets around to wherever he needs to go."

Allena smiled at the one strong leg of her grandson kicking the air and the other stretching to match it. She tickled his tummy, nuzzling his nose with hers. "And that's all legs are for, isn't it?" She kissed his forehead.

Again, Mary Lou's admiration for her mother-in-law grew. Like Mama, she had captured an open secret from God to learn from Him what to do, especially in dire times of need. "God told me" had been the answer Mama had given Pa many times.

Days flew by, chewing precious time from the month of December. Needles hurriedly assembled garments, and hammer blows resounded from the barn in preparation for Christmas day. Hattie spent the last week preparing special food.

Mary Lou's thoughts carried her back to Kansas, their little church in Venture, and the Christmas party on Christmas Eve. Her childhood remembrance of that event created an intense desire for the opportunity to build a treasure of memories for her own children—an anchor to let them know where they came from and a vision of where they were going. Perhaps, next year when the church was built. . . .

Two days before Christmas, Tom appeared at the door with a pine tree. He had pounded some boards on the bottom of the trunk so it would stand up.

"It's wonderful!" Mary Lou held back the urge to throw her arms around him, too shy with everyone present.

Mary Lou and Laura used ribbons of all colors and tied them into bows to trim the tree. They bought some popcorn from an Indian and strung red holly berries and popped corn on thread and draped it around the tree.

All was ready by three o'clock Christmas Eve. The Shepards came in two wagons. Will, Emily, Luke, and John in one, Matthew and Mark with their wives in the second. Each came in, arms full of food and presents.

The men gathered in the parlor around the fireplace and discussed their ranches and plans for the future. The women hustled an early supper to the table, surrounded with babies in new high chairs.

The longstanding neighborliness and friendship of the Shepard and Langdon families reminded Mary Lou so much of home. Will, as father, played Santa Claus. He dug into a big, mysterious bag and pulled out one present after another wrapped in brown paper or newspaper with red and white store string.

A tiny white dress for Beth from Emily, a cloth doll from her grandmother, and a fancy bib from Laura and Nelson. Wooden blocks, a toy wagon, and carved horses for the little boys. New bonnets and handkerchiefs with tatted edges for the ladies, Mary Lou's shirts for Zack, Tom, and Nelson—there seemed no bottom to Santa's bag!

When all the presents were opened, Tom took Mary Lou's hand and led her outside to a wagon standing just beyond the hitching post. He hopped up onto the wagon bed and pulled Mary Lou up beside him. A horse blanket covered something. Grinning, Tom yanked the horse blanket off the top.

Mary Lou's mouth dropped open. Her beautiful, black iron cookstove! She ran her hands over it again. This time, it belonged to her!

"And it is all ready to be taken home after dinner and hooked up to the stovepipe!" Tom threw the blanket over the stove again, leaped down, and held his arms out for Mary Lou.

She jumped into his arms. A swelling of love almost

smothered her. "It is the very one I wanted. How did you know?"

"You don't ask Santa Claus how he knows such things. It is his business to know." Tom held her close and whispered in her ear. "I never tell anyone Santa's secrets."

Hattie came out the kitchen door, went over to the bell, and rang it with gusto.

Smitty and the cowboys came from the bunkhouse, all clean and shaved, and joined the two families for Christmas supper.

Zack rose from his chair and stuck his thumbs in his vest pockets. "As I look about, I cannot help but think this is what we are all working for and what Christmas is all about. Peace on earth and good will to men. And we understand a little better this year how much we need God's peace.

"We think of our brother," Zack lowered his head and swallowed hard, "who is missing around this table." He choked up and turned to Tom. "Will you say grace, please?" Zack sat down.

Tom stood quietly. "Father, we thank You for the gift of a Savior born that night long ago to save us from our sins. Thank You for our families and friends and these cowboys who work hard with us." He paused. "We thank You for this bounty of food before us and ask You to bless it in Jesus' name. Amen."

Dusk descended early. After a merry day and a delicious Christmas supper, the Shepards climbed aboard their wagons with their gifts and were waved on their way. Later, Tom and Mary Lou boarded their wagon and started home, followed by Tex and Bart on horseback to help put the stove in place.

Mary Lou sat beside Tom, a drowsy, blanket-wrapped twin in each arm. She gazed up at the dark winter sky spattered with tiny stars faithfully maintaining their vigil. What must it have been like for the shepherds that special night when that bright star led them to Jesus in Bethlehem? They probably never knew the significance of their faithful visit.

She pulled the blanket tighter around her babies. "And she wrapped him in swaddling clothes and laid him in a manger." For the first time, Mary Lou realized how Mary must have felt for the safety of her son. And Joseph, who had the burden of their care and safety, just like Tom. The importance of each detail in the beloved Christmas story flooded her with deeper understanding.

The wagon rolled to a stop in front of their house. Tom took the twins, and Tex helped Mary Lou down from the wagon. By the time the twins were tucked in their beds and Mary Lou came out into the kitchen, the stove stood in place. The men were hooking up the stovepipe. As soon as it was finished, Tex and Bart called "Merry Christmas" and rode off.

Tom took her in his arms and said in a deep, throaty voice, "Merry Christmas, darling." He bent his head until his lips touched hers.

Mama said heaven was much more than anyone dreamed of, Mary Lou thought. *Could it possibly be much better than this?*

twenty-one

Allena, Hattie, and Laura came to visit Mary Lou three days after Christmas to see how the stove worked, so they planned to eat supper together.

The women brought their own dishes since Mary Lou didn't have enough to serve everyone. They also brought their food in pans to cook on the top of her cookstove. Hattie brought dry biscuit makings to mix with water later and bake in the oven.

They were all impressed with the five-gallon water vat on the side of the stove where water could be stored and kept hot all the time. Hattie got a fire started in the fire pit, commenting about the small pieces of wood that could be used and how easy it was to carry them. She kept picking up the circular lids with the handle to see how the fire was burning, like some child with a new toy.

Mary Lou had a hard time keeping Tom's surprise to herself. Tom had told her that when he bought her stove, he had ordered one for his mother and Hattie.

For Mary Lou, it was a joy to have company for supper in their new home. As they ate, they decided to make it a habit to have supper at Tom and Mary Lou's every Saturday evening.

By April, the days warmed up and stirred homeward thoughts in Mary Lou's mind. The morning Tom rode out on the spring roundup, he kissed her, held her in his arms, and said, "As soon as the roundup is over, we will begin the trip to Kansas. Will you be ready?"

Ready! She had been waiting for those words. Mary Lou enveloped Tom in a smothering hug and lingering kiss. For the first time, she waved him off gladly.

From then on, Kansas and home was all Mary Lou thought about. Her mind buzzed with ideas of how to travel with the twins, what needs they would have, how long it would take.

Allena's concern for the babies was the daily exposure to the hot sun or rain. Tom solved that problem by soaking thin pieces of wood in water and then bending and tying them until they dried in a curved shape. He used the shaped wood as stays covered with canvas to form a shelter in the back of the wagon, making it look like a miniature Conestoga.

Mary Lou packed two wooden buckets to scoop water from rivers or ponds. Tom strapped a water barrel on the side of the wagon between the wheels.

Dr. Mike stopped by one day to check the babies.

Hattie smiled. "That's what he says he comes for, but I think his stomach is crying out for a good, home-cooked meal."

Dr. Mike's appetite proved her right.

"Have you any news of Lily?" Allena asked.

"There are rumors she left town with some man, but no one seemed to know who or where or why. It's just a rumor, and Allena, you know you can't count on everything you hear. It has been going around, so by now it's probably far from the truth."

Allena shook her head. "That can't be true. Somehow I

can't believe that of Lily."

Mary Lou didn't either—unless Lily had backslidden.

A couple days later, Zack came home in the middle of the day for dinner, which he hadn't done since baby Zack was a newborn. The family soon found out why. He had received a letter from Darcy with another offer from her father of a position in his law office.

"I can read between the lines," Zack said sadly at the dinner table. "She doesn't want to come back here to live, so the offer is an enticement for me to go back to Boston." His jaw tightened as he read parts of the letter to his family.

The news came as no surprise to Mary Lou. In each of Darcy's letters, she had given reasons why she needed to stay in Boston a little longer. Mary Lou had pushed her thought aside and never voiced what she had sensed all along. Darcy had never intended to come back.

"This Zack isn't the Zack I married," she had said.

But what about baby Zack? Doesn't every mother love her own baby? Evidently not. Mary Lou remembered at the baby's birth when Allena laid Darcy's newborn son in her arms. "Take it away!" Darcy had cried. It! Was that all her baby was to her? Darcy had rejected both son and father.

Tom returned from the spring roundup and preparations for going to Kansas became the daily chore. Mary Lou gathered her bags of dried vegetables and meat. Allena gave a metal tin for flour, and they made a batch of sourdough starter so Mary Lou could fry bread in a frying pan over an open fire.

The excitement of seeing Pa, Aunt Nelda, Aunt Tibby, and Jenny made Mary Lou yearn to push each day ahead of itself.

Laura rode in one morning before they planned to leave. "That wagon's not going to hold much more," she commented.

"That's what Tom said this morning. Yet I have a feeling I'm forgetting something, but I can't remember what." Staring at Laura, Nelson came to mind. "Nelson's paintings! I have forgotten Nelson's paintings!"

"I wondered whether you remembered," Nelson said when they went to see him. "Thought maybe you didn't have room."

"We'll make room!"

Nelson had already selected pictures he thought were particularly good. Those of Father Zack and Victor he refused to part with. Mary Lou didn't blame him. They were priceless.

There were many pictures of tumbleweeds. They selected the best of those. Choosing the best of the cowboy paintings was difficult. They shifted them from the "go" pile to the "stay" pile several times until they felt they had culled the best. One exceptional painting of Smitty holding Diamond, Nelson refused to part with. By the time they finished, they had sifted out the best portraits and landscapes and had enough variety to make them interesting.

Allena brought muslin bags she had made to protect them.

"I'm sure there will be some place in Pa's store where he can hang them," Mary Lou said. "We will take some to Abilene. There are lots of people there." She pointed to Nelson's signature. "Did you have that on there before?"

"No, Mr. Dillard told me that every artist signs his work,

and he showed me how when he was here the last time. It took me a while to sign them all, but I did." Nelson looked up with a satisfied grin.

"We did," Laura corrected.

Nelson laughed. "She's right. It gave her an excuse to go through all my things and clean the room. So, while she was handling every picture, she brought them to me to sign." Nelson's gaze crossed the room and caressed her. "Otherwise, it would have taken me forever and I would never have known which I signed and which I didn't."

There were fourteen pictures. Laura and Mary Lou slipped each one in a muslin bag and then bunched paintings of like sizes together and tied them with small rope.

The day of departure finally came.

"I want to start about five-thirty in the morning," Tom said. "That will get us across the Red River and hopefully well up into Indian territory before nightfall."

Good-byes are always hard. Hugs, choked tears, and kisses were given as if it were the last time. In the back of every mind, though no one said so, it could be. Crossing through Indian territory was sometimes safe and sometimes not. Most Indians were friendly and curious. Some were not. Just like white men.

Allena and Hattie each held a twin until the last minute. Reluctantly they handed them up to Mary Lou who settled one in each arm. Tom had built the seat back taller so the twins could sit between their parents and not fall back into the wagon.

Finally Tom slapped the reins on the horses' backs, the wagon creaked, and the wheels slowly rolled forward.

Mary Lou couldn't wave for risk of losing a twin. One quick look back was enough. All three women were crying. Zack stood waving his arm. Nelson stood tall and smiled.

Mary Lou turned her face to her husband. The wagon was rolling now and he glanced into her eyes.

"Mrs. Langdon, you keep praying and I'll keep driving and we'll get there in good shape."

Excitement and fear fought in Mary Lou's stomach. She didn't remember being this afraid when they had come from Kansas. The ecstasy of being Tom's wife precluded everything.

Her mind shot home. An old fear revived. Had Pa forgiven her? Would he accept Tom now? Would he speak to her at all?

Pray for yourselves and your father as you go. God is with you. That's what Mama would have advised. Mary Lou's frantic heart eased. Her eyes rested on Tom's capable hands, tightly gripped over the reins. She glanced at the babies in her arms.

The sun fanned forth golden spears that flooded their way with sunshine.

"This is the day the Lord has made. Let us rejoice and be glad in it," Mary Lou said and turned a smiling face to Tom.

"And we will do just that."

A Letter To Our Readers

Dear Reader:

In order that we might better contribute to your reading enjoyment, we would appreciate your taking a few minutes to respond to the following questions. When completed, please return to the following:

Karen Carroll, Editor
Heartsong Presents
P.O. Box 719
Uhrichsville, Ohio 44683

1. Did you enjoy reading *Rainbow Harvest*?
   - ☐ Very much. I would like to see more books
     by this author!
   - ☐ Moderately
     I would have enjoyed it more if _____

   _____

2. Are you a member of *Heartsong Presents*? Yes   No
   If no, where did you purchase this book? _____

   _____

3. What influenced your decision to purchase
   this book? (Circle those that apply.)

Cover	Back cover copy
Title	Friends
Publicity	Other _____

4. On a scale from 1 (poor) to 10 (superior), please rate the following elements.

    ___Heroine   ___Plot

    ___Hero   ___Inspirational theme

    ___Setting   ___Secondary characters

5. What settings would you like to see covered in *Heartsong Presents* books?

_____

_____

6. What are some inspirational themes you would like to see treated in future books?_____

_____

_____

7. Would you be interested in reading other *Heartsong Presents* titles?   Yes   No

8. Please circle your age range:

Under 18	18-24	25-34
35-45	46-55	Over 55

9. How many hours per week do you read? _____

Name _____

Occupation _____

Address _____

City _____ State _____ Zip _____

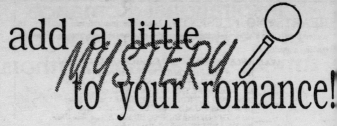

Inspirational Romance at its Best from one of America's Favorite Authors!

FOUR HISTORICAL ROMANCES
BY COLLEEN L. REECE

___ *A Torch for Trinity*—When Trinity Mason sacrifices her teaching ambitions for a one-room school, her life—and Will Thatcher's—will never be the same. HP1 BHSB-01 $2.95

___*Candleshine*-A sequel to *A Torch for Trinity*—With the onslaught of World War II, Candleshine Thatcher dedicates her life to nursing, and then her heart to a brave Marine lieutenant. HP7 BHSB-06 $2.95

___*Wildflower Harvest*—Ivy Ann and Laurel were often mistaken for each other...was it too late to tell one man the truth? HP2 BHSB-02 $2.95

___ *Desert Rose*-A sequel to *Wildflower Harvest*—When Rose Birchfield falls in love with one of Michael's letters, and then with a cowboy named Mike, no one is more confused than Rose herself. HP8 BHSB-08 $2.95